21st September 2019

Dear hi

Best wishes,

[signature] x

2012
THE SYMPHONY
A novel about global transformation

ANGELA CLARKE

Lumière Publishing

2012
THE SYMPHONY
A novel about global transformation

Angela Clarke
© Angela Clarke 2011

Published by Lumière Publishing
48 Sudlow Road London
SW18 1HP United Kingdom
www.lumiereassociates.com

PAPERBACK ISBN: 978-1-908151-00-1

HARDCOVER ISBN: 978-1-908151-06-3

E-BOOK ISBN: 978-1-908151-01-8

SECOND EDITION
(INCLUDES NEW MATERIAL, 80 EXTRA PAGES)
First published by 1st World Publishing December 2008

The right of Angela Clarke to be identified as the author of this work has been asserted in accordance with the Copyright Designs and Patents Act 1988. No part of this book may be reproduced or used by any means without permission in writing from the author. This book is a work of fiction, and any resemblance to actual persons either living or dead is coincidental. The work as been written and published solely for educational purposes. The author and publisher shall have neither liability nor responsibility to any person or entity with respect to any loss, damage or injury caused or alleged to be caused directly or indirectly by the information contained in this book.

To my mother Anne, who has always been an inspiration to me, and my father Ron, who encouraged me to see beyond the status quo.

Foreword

According to the Mayans, 2012 heralds the end of a 26,000 year evolutionary cycle. The end of the world as we know it. The start of a new Golden Age.

When I first heard about 2012, my curiosity was aroused, and I started reading everything I could find on the subject. I read fiction, nonfiction, and everything in between, experiencing the extremes of exhaustive research and hallucinogenic hypothesis.

What I read inspired me to write a novel in which the characters have a similar journey to my own. They are intelligent, seemingly rational people who start to question their long-held beliefs, drivers, and motivations once they start to see beyond the illusion of a society focused on materialism, social position, and self-interest.

A key aspect of their transition is a reconnection with nature and a realization of the intrinsic connection between all human beings. As part of that journey, they become aware of the importance of music and its contribution to the profound reawakening of consciousness all over the world.

Many of the ideas explored by the book are drawn from historical fact or scientific research, and the references to scientists, websites, books and research are all factual. However, the reader is encouraged to do their own research to test any hypothesis. Indeed, one of the underlying themes of the novel is the importance of questioning what others tell us and coming to our own conclusions.

Current world events play a significant part in the novel, from the "credit crunch" to the effects of climate change. The novel places the reader in the context of the challenges he is facing today and suggests possible ways to overcome them. In fact, the book suggests that some of today's challenges have been orchestrated by a powerful "global elite," whose long-term agenda has been to maintain absolute control and keep humanity from becoming empowered in order to pursue its own self-serving goals.

While writing this book, my rational mind was in constant debate with my intuitive mind. When in an intuitive state, the concepts inspired me. When in a rational state, everything sounded irrational.

You may have the same experience while reading it. Whatever you do, try to think outside the square. It's something we all struggle with. The familiarity of long-held beliefs provides a relative safety net that may not be as safe as we think. The status quo is a very compelling place to be, mainly because everybody else is there too. That doesn't mean to say it's right.

Angela Clarke

PROLOGUE

Meeting of the Nine

Oxfordshire, United Kingdom, December 2007

The Rolls-Royce Phantom purred along the country lane, taking up almost the entire road as it followed the rays of the setting sun. Its distinguished, middle-aged passenger, known as "The Master," took a sip of whisky before leaning back on the headrest, planning what he would say at the meeting.

Suddenly, the chauffeur slowed down and turned left, driving up the long, secluded drive, arriving within a few minutes at the front door of the imposing Manor House. A butler opened the car door and ushered him into the entry hall, taking his coat. "Good evening sir. They are waiting for you in the drawing room."

He walked into the drawing room, where eight other men were gathered around a roaring fire, some standing, others seated on comfortable sofas or leather wingback chairs. "Welcome to the Manor," said the man sitting in the chair next to the fireplace. "Brown, can you organize the drinks then leave us? We won't need you any further this evening." The butler quietly served the last drinks, then discreetly left the room, closing the heavy wooden doors behind him.

The Master walked over to the fireplace and took a cigar from the cigar box on the mantelpiece. Slowly and deliberately, he sniffed it, rolled it in his fingers next to his ear, and cut the end off with a cigar cutter. Then he lit it, before turning to face the group. "The Great Transition is approaching," he said, "and we need to intensify our strategy. Our efforts to disillusion and crush our opponents have only seen a 40% rate of success."

"The Light Ones are getting stronger by adversity," he continued grimly. "More of them are awakening to who they are, and are forming alliances and groups. Many of them are women, who will tip the balance of control away from us. The new energies are streaming through more powerfully than ever. If we are not vigilant, this will influence and lead humanity to realize its true power. It could destroy us."

The man sitting on the leather chair next to the fire cleared his throat before speaking. "We are succeeding, however, in keeping the people in a state of fear. My media companies only ever report bad news. Our advertising has driven them into a frenzy of materialistic consumerism. As long as they remain in fear, powerless to change anything, and focused on external sources of gratification, they won't be receptive to the new information."

"I agree," said the man on the sofa. "Many also still operate within a 'pack' mentality, and most are still completely guided by social and peer influences. Our strategy to keep them focused on personal gratification under the guise of more genuine forms of 'New Age' self-empowerment has also been enormously successful. My appointed 'spiritual teachers' are leading more and more gullible followers to our Way, under the guise of true enlightenment." He smiled, his eyes cold and calculating. "It is quite amusing to watch."

The man sitting next to him nodded. "The food additives and poisons they have been ingesting for years have damaged their health and reproductive ability. The current food crisis will facilitate widespread use of genetically modified foods. Drugs, violence, and childhood abuse have ruined countless young lives."

The man standing near the window turned around. "Importantly," he added, "our strategy to destabilize the world economy is working. We have made millions by buying up cheap assets. The people will welcome tighter controls after this debacle."

"Our policies in the Middle East have inflamed the extremists and facilitated our move towards a surveillance society," added another.

The Master roared with anger. "You are all asleep! Can't you see the signs of change? They are all around us. They are waking up to our agenda. Our success has always been based on keeping ourselves hidden from view. Keeping them in ignorance, confusion, in fear of social and peer group opinions. Fostering their desire for even more material consumption. Keeping them constantly warring against each other, so that they don't have time to realize their true enemy."

"This time, it is different from Atlantis," he continued. We succeeded that time because they were so consumed with arrogance that they did not heed the signs. There are more Light Ones now, and they are far more militant. The energies are more powerful. Information on the Internet and in the field of collective consciousness is doubling every split second. They are becoming aware."

"The polar shift takes place on December 21, 2012. We only have a few short years to keep them from taking power." The Master walked to the door of the drawing room. "I am flying back to New York later tonight. By the time I arrive in my office tomorrow morning, I expect to see your new strategies on my desk. Good evening, gentlemen."

PART ONE

THE AWAKENING

I tell you that the children of yesteryear are walking in the funeral of the era which they created for themselves. They are pulling a rotting rope that may break soon and cause them to drop into a forgotten abyss. I say that they are living in homes with weak foundations. As the storm blows- and it is about to blow - their homes will fall upon their heads and thus become their tombs. I say that all their thoughts, their sayings, their quarrels, their compositions, their books and all their works are nothing but chains dragging them because they are too weak to pull the load.

But the children of tomorrow are the ones called by life, and they follow it with steady steps and heads high. They are the dawn of the new frontiers; no smoke will veil their eyes and no jingle of chains will drown out their voices. They are few in number but the difference is as between a grain of wheat and a stack of hay. No one knows them but they know each other. They are like the summits, which can see and hear each other- not like caves, which cannot hear or see. They are the seed dropped by the hand of God in the field, breaking through its pod and waving its sapling leaves before the face of the sun. It shall grow into a mighty tree; its roots in the heart of the Earth and its branches high in the sky.

— Kahlil Gibran

Chapter 1

Escape to Mexico…

Aurelie awoke from her slumber lulled by the sound of ocean waves crashing on the beach. She felt a growing sense of elation as she gazed around the room, admiring the polished wooden furniture splashed with vibrant color, and picture windows opening onto a glorious sandy beach.

They had arrived in Cancun the night before, exhausted from a long flight from Paris, and had been chauffeured to their luxury resort on the Riviera Maya. Jules, whose strong, tanned body was spread out on the bed beside her, was gently snoring. Sighing, she rolled over and wrapped the silky Egyptian cotton sheet around her shoulders, shutting her eyes to capture a little more sleep.

After a few minutes, Aurelie decided she couldn't stay in bed any longer. She jumped up and walked into the bathroom, grabbing one of the fluffy white towels on the side of the bed. To her surprise, there was an outdoor shower beyond the indoor one.

She went outside, turned on the water and closed her eyes, enjoying the feeling of warm water and a light breeze caressing her body. *I am so glad to be here*, she thought as the sun warmed her skin.

Suddenly, she felt a pair of hands rubbing her back in a slow rhythmical motion. Jules kissed her on the back of the neck and then pulled her around to face him. She was filled with joy at that moment, and kissed him wetly on the mouth, before pushing him away and grabbing a towel to wrap around her.

Aurelie walked over to the bathroom vanity and stared at herself in the mirror. The past 12 months had been exhausting both emotionally and physically, and it showed. Dark circles were apparent under her eyes and her skin looked drab and pale. *God I look terrible*!

Aurelie had left her law firm last month and was unemployed for the first time in fifteen years. After five years with the firm, it had been her turn to be granted partner status, but they had bypassed her for a younger, less senior, and in her opinion less competent man.

Part of her wasn't surprised at the decision, because she had never been part of the male "club" culture within the firm. The only female partner just about survived, but only because she played the "dumb blonde" despite her clever mind and outstanding record of legal wins. Aurelie was more straightforward and couldn't play politics, so many of them disliked her.

There was also the billing issue. Aurelie had discovered that one of her major clients, a children's charity, was being overcharged and she threatened to tell them the truth if the firm didn't stop exploiting them. Although the president fully supported her, the financial controller was outraged that she had exposed him.

Needless to say, he wasted no time in turning the partners against her. She remembered the day they told her very clearly. A meeting was being held in the upstairs boardroom between the existing partners. There were four hopefuls, but only three were to be chosen. She drew comfort in the fact that she had been there for the longest and had a faultless record.

After the meeting, Laurent called her into his office. "They didn't choose you," he said grimly. "What on earth did you do to the partners for them to hate you so much?"

The same day, she wrote her letter of resignation and went straight home. Standing out on her balcony, she lit a cigarette. *What am I going to do?* she asked herself. *My career is in ruins. Every sacrifice I've ever made, all wasted. All the relationships I neglected because my job came first. What a waste of a life.*

Her affair with Laurent, one of the partners, was over as well. It wasn't ever something she could talk about, anyway, because it was strictly against the rules in the firm. But everybody was doing it, it just wasn't public knowledge. She had really loved Laurent, or thought she did, but he didn't see her as wife material.

When he ended up marrying a hairdresser from his hometown of Marseille, she resigned herself to the fact that brains and beauty were not enough for some men. In fact, they were too much for the men she had known.

Jules was a 23-year-old law student she had met in a bar one night. They got drunk and he came home to her plush apartment in the 5th arrondissement that first night, and had wonderful sex. Although she had only known him a few weeks, she took him on holiday to Mexico the week after she left the firm. He looked up to her, and she needed someone to adore her at the moment. It made up for the way she felt about herself.

"*On y va?*"[1] Jules' question jolted her out of her reverie. She finished brushing her glossy dark-blonde hair and applied some concealer under her eyes. *A tan will fix that up in no time.* She grabbed his hand and they walked across the beach to the restaurant, where they were given a prime table on the terrace facing the ocean.

---

1 Shall we go?

Chapter 2

After a few days at the resort, Aurelie had started to unwind and relax. She was stretched out on the soft, spongy beach bed, sheltered from the sun by a large beach umbrella. Jules appeared suddenly, diving onto the bed. "You should have come surf skiing, it was fantastic," he said, before rolling on top of her, still completely wet. "Get off me," she said as she shrieked with laughter. "I'd rather conserve my energy for the Temazcal tonight."

Just before 5pm that afternoon, Aurelie and Jules walked hand in hand over to pyramid-shaped structure set on the beach, where the Temazcal, a traditional Mayan cleansing ceremony, was to be performed. They were greeted by a petite Mexican woman who asked them to sit down to wait for the others.

When the other six people had arrived, Julia, who introduced herself as the "shaman", asked them to enter the underground pyramid and sit down in front of a pile of steaming hot volcanic rocks. As the doors closed behind them and darkness set in, Aurelie felt a growing sense of apprehension. She reached out her hand to Jules, and he squeezed it reassuringly. Then the shaman began to chant and sing, encouraging them all to join in.

As they all chanted, Aurelie felt herself drift away into a dreamlike state. In her mind's eye, she found herself at the edge of what looked like a huge well, gazing into the water's depths. There seemed to be something living in the water.

Sssssssssssssss............the sound of water splashing on the hot stones jolted her back to reality. "Please, look into the stones and tell me what animal you see," said the shaman. "This ancient ritual has been practiced by the Mayans for centuries. The kind of animal you see will explain what you are here to cleanse or understand."

Aurelie stared hard into the stones. She couldn't really see anything except for a few glowing embers. After a few minutes, she thought she could see something. Was it a turtle? Just as the heat became completely unbearable, the doors were opened. "Now run to the ocean to wash the energies from you," said the shaman. "When you return, I will tell you the meaning of the animal you saw in the hot stones and give you a cup of cleansing tea."

They ran to the ocean and dived in, then bobbed up and down in the waves. Aurelie felt a sense of release as they splashed and laughed with the others. They walked back to the stone terrace, outside the pyramid, where Julia handed them a cup of delicious spicy tea. She went through the meanings of every animal with all the others. When she came to Aurelie, her voice lowered.

"Aurelie, you have chosen the Turtle. The Turtle is the oldest symbol for planet Earth."

"It is the personification of goddess energy and the eternal Mother from which our lives evolve," she continued. "Turtle has a shell like Mother Earth, which protects herself in the form of Earth changes, volcanoes, and climate alterations. Turtle teaches you how to use protection, honor the creative source within you, and ground yourself."

"It asks you to use the water and earth energies, Turtle's two homes, to flow harmoniously with your situation and place your feet firmly on the ground in a power stance. Turtle buries its thoughts, like eggs in the sand. This teaches you to develop your ideas before you bring them into the light. If you draw the Turtle card, it reminds you to connect with the power of Earth and the Mother-Goddess within. Ask for her assistance, and abundance will follow."

As they thanked Julia for the ceremony, she whispered to Aurelie. "I must speak to you in private. I will bring the Turtle scroll to your room later this evening."

Aurelie and Jules walked in silence along the beach back to their bungalow, awed by the experience. After a light room service dinner, they curled up together on the sofa, listening to the waves crash on the beach. Suddenly, there was a light tap on the door. Aurelie jumped up to open it, and invited Julia to come in.

She got straight to the point. "It is no accident that you have come to the Yucatan at this time. There is important work to be done, and you have the choice to be part of it. A group of Elders is meeting at the 'Sacred Cenote' at Chichen Itza tomorrow afternoon." She pressed something into her hands. "Take this crystal and go to this meeting. You will understand why when you get there. Buena suerte."

Intrigued, Aurelie rang the concierge and hired a car for the next day. Although they had planned to spend the day on a yacht, something told her that she should go. She wasn't sure what a Cenote was but she knew it would be signposted when she arrived.

That night, Aurelie dreamed of diving into a beautiful blue green underground pool, illuminated by a beam of light from above. As she rose to the surface, she saw an amazing display of tree roots and stalactites hanging from above. She climbed out and sat on the limestone rocks, gazing at the water, which seemed to be vibrating with energy.

Chapter 3

The next day, Aurelie and Jules set off in their hired car. They left at 8.30 with a packed picnic from the hotel, having decided to see the Mayan ruins at Tulum on the way. As they wandered around the ancient walled city, Aurelie stopped in front of El Castillo, perched right on the edge of the cliff overlooking the turquoise sea. "Look at those amazing plumed serpents," she said to Jules. She felt a strange sense of déjà vu.

After a quick swim in the ocean, they walked back to their car and set off for Chichen Itza. They drove across the peninsula through miles and miles of jungle, before hitting another main highway that took them straight to the ancient Mayan city.

Although the day had started gloriously, the sky started to darken with storm clouds as they came closer to their destination. "I hope the weather holds out," said Jules. They parked outside, and walked through the imposing entrance into the ancient city.

"Chichen Itza is one of the New Seven Wonders of the world," said Aurelie, as they walked around in awe, admiring the temples and palaces surrounded by dense jungle. They stopped and gazed up at the pyramid of Kukulkan towering above them.

Jules stared at the guidebook in his hands. "Apparently, there are 365 steps in total to this temple, one for every day of the year. On the spring and autumn equinox," he added, "the shadow of the sun on the stairs causes the illusion of a snake descending the pyramid in the direction of the Cenote - which is an underground well, located down that road." He gazed at Aurelie. "Even the word Chichen means 'mouth of the well,' according to this guide. Sounds like it is the main reason they built the city here."

Aurelie felt a shiver run down her spine. "Let's go and see the Cenote," she said, walking quickly towards the dirt road.

Chapter 4

Reuters.... April 4th, 2008: Yasmin da Souza, Environmental advisor to the Brazilian Government, has resigned, claiming she was losing the battle against big business in her attempts to protect the Amazon, otherwise known as the "lungs of the planet." In her letter to President Marco Fernandez, de Souza said that her department was continuously being thwarted by forces within government and business who were more interested in Brazil's economic development than conserving the environment.

The Green Movement's office in Sao Paolo was buzzing at the news. CEO Jonathan Marshall called his friend Mike Savage, President of World Canopy in New York. "This is a disaster," he said. "The final straw probably came when Fernandez approved the new road and dam-building project in the Amazon basin. I don't blame her, really, but what on earth will we do now?"

Mike thought for a few minutes. "Actually, it could be the best thing to have happened. Fernandez can no longer claim a green policy and hide behind her credentials. We need to meet with her to discuss the next steps. She has access to insider information that will help us in tackling this more effectively."

Yasmin was lying in the bath at her beachside apartment in Buzios, north of Rio. It was a long way from the shack in the favela where she grew up. She felt a sense of relief, combined with frustration, at the events of yesterday. She couldn't believe that after everything she had explained to him, Fernandez still went ahead and approved that dam project. It was all too much - she wasn't getting anywhere.

They were too strong, too powerful. Short-term greed and financial gain were their only considerations. Enough was enough.

Suddenly, the phone rang shrilly. Reluctantly, she stood up and grabbed her robe before walking out into the hallway. *It could be important.*

"Olá? Good afternoon, this is Mike Savage from World Canopy."

"Hello Mike," she replied.

"Sorry for calling out of the blue, Yasmin, but first I wanted to say how sorry I was about what has happened."

"You know the situation, Mike," she said. "I didn't have much choice in the end. They are determined to go ahead with their projects—there is too much money at stake. A lot of it probably personal as well."

Mike winced. "It always ends up being about money, doesn't it? Listen, Yasmin, do you think you would be available to fly to New York within the next 2 weeks for a meeting with all the

Green movements? I can get everybody together, just give me a date."

"Of course, I would be delighted," replied Yasmin. "I'm actually flying to Mexico for a holiday on Thursday, so I can catch a direct flight to New York from Cancun. What about the week after next? "That sounds perfect," he replied. "See you in a couple of weeks—and have a well-deserved break!"

Chapter 5

The plane from Miami to Cancun was packed with noisy young Americans, escorted by a couple of older people who looked as exhausted as she felt. *Probably some kind of school excursion*, she thought as she fell back into a light sleep, wishing the trip would soon be over.

A cabin announcement jolted Yasmin awake. She got up and walked to the back of the plane, discovering to her dismay that there was a queue for the toilet. Yasmin stared at the door, wondering what on earth the person was doing in there for so long.

A pleasant-looking woman behind her struck up conversation. "Hello, my name is Conchita," she said.

"Yasmin," she replied briefly, not wanting to talk.

The woman's brow furrowed. "You are involved in very important work," she continued, "and this work is now in danger. You must be very careful, the world's future is at stake."

Yasmin looked at her in astonishment. "Why are you telling me this?" she asked. "What do you know about me? Who are you?"

"I am a friend," the woman answered quietly. "You must visit Chichen Itza whilst you are in Mexico," she continued. "If you value your work, and your mission in life, then you will go."

The door of the toilet suddenly swung open, and a pale-looking woman came out. It was Yasmin's turn, so she went in. Curious about what the woman had said, she was anxious to ask her more questions when she came out.

She hurriedly flushed the toilet, washed her hands, and came out, but there was no sign of the woman anywhere. She looked up and down the aisles of the plane, but she was nowhere to be seen. She went back to her seat and fell asleep, waking up only when the plane landed.

Yasmin checked in to her hotel, looking forward to collapsing on the beach and catching up on some well-earned sleep. Once in her room, she changed into her swimming costume, grabbed a book, and walked down to the pool where she planned to spend the entire day relaxing and reading. She left her mobile in the room to make sure she wouldn't be disturbed.

Finding a vacant lounge chair next to the huge swimming pool, Yasmin laid out her towel and stretched out. She started reading the book that she had picked up at the airport, a novel written by a popular American author. *Oh well*, she thought. *I need some escapism, even if it's a load of mindless rubbish.*

After reading for a while, Yasmin's mind drifted back to what the woman on the plane had said. *I suppose it wouldn't hurt to go and take a look*, she thought. *I was planning to go to the ruins anyway, and Chichen Itza is apparently the most important, even though it's about three hours away.* She made a mental resolve to book a car there for the next day.

Early that evening, Yasmin sat on her terrace with a glass of wine, enjoying the cool breeze that was coming from the ocean. *The biggest decision I have to make today is what restaurant to dine in*, she smiled to herself. *I really needed this break, after everything that has happened.*

Yasmin dressed and went down to dinner in the resort's seafood restaurant. She was given a small table near the bar, overlooking the beach. "Are you dining alone?" asked the waiter politely. "Yes," she replied. *I'm all alone*, she thought. *Always have been, probably always will be.*

Yasmin had been single most of her life. Her harsh upbringing in the Rio favelas did nothing to ingratiate her to the vagaries of married life. A father that beat them and then abandoned them, a mother who tried her best but couldn't really cope with life at all.

Yasmin had decided, at the age of 12, never to be dependent on any man. She would never put herself in the same position as her mother had been. She would always be self-sufficient, and able to walk away if a man treated her badly.

The problem was that she had set herself up so successfully that no man ever dared enter her world. Not that she was still a virgin, of course. She had had her fair share of experiences when she was younger, but none of them had really satisfied her. They were always with unavailable men, so she inevitably ended up feeling hurt.

Yasmin sighed. *Ramon was the worst*, she thought to herself. *He was just using me to get to the President. He succeeded. He is in, I am out.* Ramon was a colleague who took over the Amazon portfolio after she objected to the strategy.

She decided to have a drink at the bar before calling it a night. "Caiprihinia," she replied when the barman asked her what she wanted to drink. A handsome, olive-skinned man walked over and sat next to her at the bar. He was attending a conference in the hotel and was alone as well. After a few drinks, they started kissing passionately.

He grabbed her hand, and they walked over to the beach. Yasmin felt light-headed, almost tipsy. She felt his body press against her. She softened her body and rocked forward and back, enjoying the experience, vaguely hoping he had put on some protection. It was as if nothing mattered anymore but the here and now.

Chapter 6

It was an unusually warm April day in London and the city was overflowing with life. Penny was sitting in a riverside café with her friend Marianne, soaking up the spring sunshine and enjoying a glass of chilled white wine.

"When did you find out?" asked Marianne quietly. Penny took a deep breath before she replied. "As you know, I have suspected something was up for some time. I checked his credit card receipts and found an unexplained amount for £395." Tears started to roll down her cheeks. "I had it traced to a high-class brothel in Central London."

Marianne was stunned. Penelope was a beautiful, intelligent, willowy brunette. She had been married to John for less than a year. Why on earth was he seeing prostitutes?

"Did you confront him with it?" she asked. "Yes, but he denied it of course," replied Penny. "But the evidence is there, and I'm afraid that I can't live with this. I need to get away to work out what I am going to do."

"Why don't we go away for a couple of weeks to lie on a beach somewhere?" said Marianne. "Danny and Olivia have been begging us to visit them in Mexico for so long. What do you think?"

"Sounds wonderful," replied Penny. 'Just what I need.'

Back in Marianne's comfortable riverside apartment, Penny started to think about her options. She needed to get legal advice, because she didn't know if she had grounds to file for divorce. Money would be tight for a while. Her job as a scientific researcher was stimulating but did not pay all that well. John, a city trader, had been the major breadwinner of the household.

Penny sat down at her computer to continue working on the paper she was writing for a major scientific publication. Her mind kept drifting back to the situation with John. Why didn't he find her attractive? What was wrong with her? What had she done wrong? Her mind kept going around in circles.

Exasperated, she started to play Solitaire on the computer. *This is stupid*, she thought. *Pull yourself together*.

Penny wondered if she should ring her mother. She was dreading her reaction. She had promised John that she would not discuss with the family the reason why she had left him. What reason could she give for leaving him? The last thing she needed right now was a pep talk.

Penny's mother had put up with years of philandering from her father. As a little girl, she used to hear them arguing about his affairs in their bedroom. She never left him, though. Her mother told her that it was a different generation and that she felt powerless to do anything.

Strangely enough, she always thought her mother was the strong one and her father the weak one. *Things are not always what they seem*, she thought. It was a lesson that would serve her well, sooner than she realized.

Chapter 7

As Penny and Marianne walked out of the arrivals hall at Cancun airport, they saw Danny and Olivia smiling broadly as they walked towards them. Danny insisted on taking all their luggage as they walked over to the nearby car park.

"How was the flight?" asked Olivia as they piled into the Landrover. "Pretty tiring, but at least it was non-stop," replied Marianne. They had booked seats on a charter flight into Cancun to avoid going via Mexico City.

After a short drive on the highway, Danny turned left into an imposing hotel entrance. As deputy manager for the resort, Danny and Olivia lived in a villa on the grounds so that he could be available 24 hours a day. The car pulled up in front of a delightful thatched-roof villa not far from the beach.

"Why don't you take a shower and freshen up, and meet us at the hotel bar at around 7 pm?" said Olivia. "We have quite a treat for you this evening."

A couple of hours later, Penny and Marianne walked across the beach to the hotel bar. They felt a hundred times better than when they arrived, and were glad to feel the intense heat on their skin.

After they finished their drinks at the bar, a waiter came over to their table and asked them to follow him. A stretch of sand had been flattened, then lined by tea lights and bamboo flares, leading up to a table for four set up right next to the ocean. The sky in the background was a glorious pale pink.

What a beautiful sight, thought Penny.

The waiter picked up the bottle of chilled champagne in the ice bucket next to the table and started to pour it into the flutes. Penny and Marianne sat down in the chairs facing the ocean, with Danny and Olivia facing them.

"Beautiful," said Marianne.

"Thank you so much," added Penny.

"Entirely our pleasure," replied Danny with a smile. "It is so good to see you both. Glad you could come."

The evening's conversation led to what they were going to do while in Mexico. "You must see some of the Mayan ruins," said Olivia. "I would definitely see Tulum, as it is only about an hour from here. You can drive down to Tulum first, then over to Chichen Itza, which is another 2 to 3 hours away."

"Chichen Itza was one of the most important Mayan temples ever built, and is quite spectacular," she continued. "It is named after a huge underground well, called the Sacred Cenote. The word 'Itza' is believed to derive from the Maya word for magic, 'itz' and '(h)á' meaning water."

39

Penny gazed out to the ocean. "A magic wishing well!," she said. "Just what I need right now. But seriously, why did the Maya consider their well sacred?"

"They believe that cenotes are portals to the 'underworld'. Archaeologists have recently found the ruins of a number of underground stone temples inside some of these cenotes, and they are still baffled as to how they were built," replied Danny.

Penny looked at Marianne. "It sounds really mysterious, don't you think? Why don't we relax for a few days in the resort, then drive up there on Friday?"

Marianne smiled lazily. "Count me in! As long as I can catch a bit of sun, I'm easy."

Chapter 8

The waves crashed soothingly and rhythmically onto the tiny but exquisite beach in Llandudno, Cape Town. Trish was alone on the beach, sitting on the rocks and watching the water rise and fall, leaving millions of tiny bubbles in its wake.

She still couldn't believe that Adrian had left her, just last week. Their lives had been a perfect combination of mutual support, contentment, and shared joy in their three children and two grandchildren, all living nearby. Or so she thought. Still attractive in her early fifties, Trish had resisted the urge to hold back the ravages of time, unlike many of her friends.

His choice of girlfriend had left her shocked and bewildered as well. Adrian was working for the local tourism body and his new girlfriend, Janet, had recently joined them from Johannesburg. Young, of course, but so brash and loud. Trish wondered if she had really ever known her husband. She threw a pebble into the water. Trish was quite philosophical about life, a "New Ager," and on some level thought that this was perhaps meant to be.

It's still really painful, she thought. *Achingly painful, actually.*

Slowly and deliberately, Trish got up and started her walk back up to the house. On the way up the steep rise, she wondered why she should bother having beautiful house overlooking the ocean, if there was nobody to share it with.

I need a holiday, she thought.

Back at the house, Trish walked into her dressing room and caught sight of herself in the full-length mirror. She saw an attractive woman with a well-proportioned, shapely figure. The skin around her eyes was wrinkled from too much sun and years of laughter, and her neck was starting to show her age. *Maybe that's why he left me*, she thought.

Trish's eyes welled up with tears and her throat tightened. W*ere relationships only really based on physical appearance? Did women have a "use-by" date that expired after a certain age?* For a moment, she felt completely worthless.

Pulling herself together, Trish went into her sitting room, sat down on her comfortable sofa, and shut her eyes. After a few minutes, she opened them again, and saw a book on the Mayan ruins sitting on the coffee table. She had bought it last week but had not had time to read it properly. Leaning over, she picked it up and started leafing through it. *This is beautiful*, she thought.

She picked up the telephone and called her daughter Linda. "Darling, how are you? And the children?" Linda replied. "The children are running me ragged, Mom."

"Mexico? That sounds absolutely wonderful. School holidays end in four weeks so anytime soon is fine with us. Charles will be home just now, so I'll check with him but I don't see any problems. I'll call you later."

Chapter 9

After collecting them from Cancun airport, the chauffeured Landrover drove quickly down the main highway towards the Riviera Maya before turning into a dirt road flanked by dense green jungle, signposted Casa Agua. Trish had booked a four-bedroom villa for herself, Linda, and her grandchildren Indigo and Joshua.

The jeep pulled up in front of a pure white, thatched roofed building, surrounded by waving palm trees and facing a turquoise ocean. Indigo and Joshua immediately jumped out of the car and ran laughing towards the sea, rolling around and playing in the silky white sand.

The butler came out to help them with the bags. Trish heaved a sigh of relief. This was exactly what she needed right now. Pure pampering and relaxation, in a beautiful place.

The next morning, Trish woke up and walked downstairs to eat breakfast on the terrace. The in-house maid was preparing delicious and spicy scrambled eggs while Linda and the children helped themselves to fresh papaya juice and sliced fruit. "Morning Nana," cried the children, as she sat down at the table.

Indigo was autistic, or at least that was how the medical profession had diagnosed her inability to speak properly. She also suffered terrible tantrums and lacked concentration. As far as Trish was concerned, however, Indigo was a very special child and she felt very bonded to her.

Her younger grandchild, Joshua, was exceptionally bright and prone to saying the most unusual things, like the time when they were sitting at the back of the hall at Indigo's end of school year presentation, and Joshua whispered to her that Indigo was talking to him in his head. *Sounds like telepathy*, Trish had thought.

Trish was open to most things of an "esoteric" nature. The New Age community in Cape Town was thriving. Trish often thought that it was the influence of Table Mountain, which according to a book she had read was a key power source for spiritual energy.

Sometimes she thought there were too many egos posing as spiritual people as well. A recent workshop she had done on self-enlightenment was in her opinion little more than a blatant front for the facilitator's own self-promotion.

"Tortilla, senora?" asked the cook, who was holding a deep clay bowl filled with warm, freshly made tortillas. Trish took one out of the bowl, and started to eat the spicy scrambled eggs the cook had placed in front of her. Between mouthfuls, Linda was scolding the children gently for playing with their food. "I don't like it," said Joshua vehemently. "Just have a little more, darling, and finish your fruit. Then we can go to the pool," replied Linda, sounding slightly exasperated.

After breakfast, they grabbed some towels and walked a few steps to the pool where Linda immediately stretched out onto a sun lounger. "Children, just play for a few more minutes before you go into the pool," she pleaded. Ignoring her pleas, Indigo and Joshua dived in and started shrieking with laughter.

Trish walked a little further onto the beach and jumped onto the hammock hooked up under two shady palm trees. It was close enough to the pool to continue a conversation with Linda, although Trish was quite keen to finish the book about the Mayans that she had brought with her from Cape Town.

She looked up from her book and called over to Linda. "Darling, I'd like to go out to see the Mayan ruins while I'm here. What about you?"

Linda replied wearily. "To be honest with you Mom, I'd much rather just lie on a beach for the entire holiday. Why don't you go and take Indigo with you? The kids are much easier to manage when they aren't together."

Chapter 10

Guy Fischer sat at his desk staring at his computer. He blinked, then glanced through the full-length glass windows that framed his corner office. A bolt of lightning had struck an adjacent building, and it was raining hard. *I have to finish the report by Friday*, he thought. The direct flight he had booked for Cancun was leaving at 10.25 am on Saturday and nothing would stop him from being on it. Not even his job.

Guy had been working overtime for weeks on a reorganization strategy for J.P. Morland, following its recent buyout of rival investment bank Beal Stantons. He was completely burned out and had started to show symptoms of a recurring stress disorder, "obsessive compulsive disorder" as the doctors diagnosed it, because of the strain he was under. He knew that if he didn't get on that flight he may not be fit to do anything else for a while.

He got up and went to the kitchen to get a glass of water. He popped a small white pill onto his tongue and took a long gulp of water. *That will calm me down*, he thought. *Back to the drawing board.*

He started to feel a little drowsy, so decided to call it a night. His partner David was already at home, sitting by the fireplace sipping a glass of red wine. "How was your day?" he asked gently, knowing what a strain he had been under.

"I'm OK," replied Guy, "just dog-tired. It's pretty much complete, just needs input from the last two focus groups. I'll be finished by Friday."

He started to feel anxious again. He went into the bathroom and washed his hands and face with cold water, to stop himself from sweating, and popped another pill. *This has to stop*, he said to himself. *The holiday will fix it.*

That night, he couldn't get to sleep. He couldn't relax; he felt agitated and nervous. He finally dozed off into a shallow sleep. He woke up suddenly in the middle of the night in a panic. Rolling over, he leaned against David for comfort and was lulled back to sleep by his rhythmic breathing.

Chapter 11

On Saturday morning, Guy and David boarded their flight at Newark Airport and set off for Cancun. This was the first holiday both of them had had for months, and they were glad that it was finally happening. They had booked the luxury resort weeks ago, and had been given an upgrade because they frequently used the hotel chain for business.

The golf cart escorted them up the winding pathway to their villa, set in the middle of dense jungle near a beautiful lagoon. David walked straight through the villa to the courtyard and turned the tap on the stone bathtub filling it with warm water.

"What a way to chill out," he exclaimed.

They peeled off their clothes and stretched out in the tub, listening to the sound of the birds in the trees and the waves crashing on the beach nearby.

After a refreshing afternoon nap, they dressed and walked up to the rooftop bar, sitting down at a corner table. "Pisco Sour please," said Guy, when the waiter came up to their table. "I'll have a Martini," said David. The drinks arrived, and they sat back in their chairs and relaxed completely.

"What do you feel like doing this week?" asked David. "Just rest, or some sightseeing as well?" Guy thought for a minute. "I'd really like to see the ruins of Chichen Itza, actually. I have read so much about it. Tulum maybe as well, and a couple of the other places."

They walked into the elegant restaurant for dinner. "Did you get any feedback from J.P. Morland about your strategy?" asked David. "Nothing yet," replied Guy as he sipped on his chilled crab soup. "But there is some interesting stuff in there that may ruffle a few feathers," he added.

"You mean about the level of exposure to sub-prime?" asked David. "Yes and no," replied Guy. "Beal Stantons wasn't in such a bad shape as I thought. Sounds like it was deliberately orchestrated rumors that brought its share price down. They are in no worse shape than any of them at the moment," he continued.

"In fact, they were in better shape than J.P. Morland when they went under. So much for Beal's shareholders, and ordinary taxpayers, who have lost millions as a result. Millions that have all moved into J.P. Morland coffers," he added quietly.

David looked at him quizzically. "I thought the Fed bailed them out, along with J.P. Morland?"

"Partially, but don't forget it is still taxpayers' money," Guy replied. "They'll probably never get that money back. What puzzles me is that the Fed could have just loaned that money to Beal Stantons directly and bypassed J.P. Morland altogether, which would have kept them going. They, the shareholders and taxpayers, would all have had a better deal if they had."

"This is the tip of the iceberg," continued Guy. "The Federal Reserve and Security and Exchange Commission are looking the other way on this one. Maybe they are worried that if they look too closely, it might unravel the whole financial system. I have a feeling that too much is at stake."

Later in the week, Guy and David hired a car to go sightseeing. They set off late morning towards Chichen Itza. The temperature was already in the 90s, with not a cloud in the sky.

Chapter 12

Laurel stood in front of Intipunku, the Gateway of the Sun, and gazed down onto the spectacular ruins of Machu Picchu, which was just visible through a bed of wispy white clouds. It had been a challenging 4 days since they had set off from Cusco on the Inca Trail, walking through steep and rugged terrain and camping by the Pacamayo River.

The past 6 months had been a welcome contrast to her life in Sydney, Australia, where Laurel had been the executive producer of a well-known TV program. She had left her job because of the politics, backstabbing, and negativity that seemed to surround any senior position in the television industry.

Laurel's best friend Sam, a cameraman, was delighted when she asked him to join her on her trip to South America. Apart from being a great companion, he would be able to take some overseas footage for the TV series on permaculture and sustainable living that Laurel had decided to produce on her return.

They were both outdoors people, sporty and athletic, and it was turning out to be an incredible adventure. The trip had started in Rio de Janeiro, after a long flight from Sydney. After a few days in Rio, they had visited the glorious Iguazu Falls, which plunged into a wide gorge in a series of huge waterfalls two miles long.

Then they had flown to Buenos Aires, where they had tasted the mouth-watering Argentine beef and danced the Tango in a huge dance hall. They had soaked in hot springs in Patagonia and tasted Chilean wines in the nearby vineyards. On Easter Island they had marveled at the Moai sculptures before going diving in the Galapagos Islands.

"We made it," she said to Sam, as he put his arm around her shoulder. They walked down the long pathway into the ancient ruins, feeling as if they were both in a dream that they still had to wake from. In awe, they walked up and down the steep stone steps, taking in as much as they could before they walked out through the narrow entrance to check in to the hotel opposite the ruins.

They had decided to splurge for a night in the stylish lodge, because they wanted to attend a special shamanic ceremony that evening in the ruins that was only available for guests of the hotel.

"This is a change from the past 4 days," said Sam, as they sipped a glass of wine and relaxed in the leather chairs around the fireplace. "Tell me about it," replied Laurel. "I am so looking forward to sleeping in a proper bed tonight."

They ate a delicious meal of grilled alpaca in the restaurant overlooking the majestic valley, before grabbing a warm jacket and joining the small group of hotel guests returning to the Macchu Picchu ruins for the shamanic ceremony.

The group arrived at the Guardhouse, which had three walls, was open on one side, and was lit by several dozens of candles. A female shaman dressed in traditional Peruvian dress greeted them solemnly, and asked them to sit on the built-in stone ledge within the building.

She then began the traditional Pago a la Tierra Inca ceremony that dated back over 1,000 years. "That means 'payment to the earth,'" whispered Sam, who spoke a bit of Spanish. She started by placing several items on a white cloth that draped a table in the middle of the room, including plastic figurines, rice, and flower petals.

Then she added coca leaves dipped in wine to the pile before letting them choose an object that they could enter into the offering. Laurel chose an Inca warrior, and Sam a snake.

Meanwhile, her assistant had started a fire in a corner of the room. The shaman wrapped the pile in its cloth and held it up to the sky to whisper a small prayer, before placing it on the now blazing fire. She then sprayed the contents of a bottle of beer on the earth around the fire, while dancing around the flames.

Laurel gazed into the fire and thought she saw an ancient face, wearing a warrior type of headdress. *I must be going mad*, she thought.

The ceremony ended as the embers of the fire went out. Thanking the shaman, the group walked slowly and silently back to the hotel. Exhausted after their long day, Laurel and Sam fell asleep the moment their heads hit the pillow.

Chapter 13

The next morning, as they were sitting at breakfast, Laurel saw the shaman sitting outside on the other side of the road. She was staring at them, as if she was waiting for them to come out.

"Sam, I'm just going to pop outside to speak to her," said Laurel. "I'll come with you," he said. They walked out of the lodge and stood at the entrance, looking over at the woman.

The shaman got up and walked across the road. "Follow me," she whispered. "There is something important you must know. We can sit over here in the café."

Laurel and Sam sat down, and looked at her expectantly. "Are you going to Mexico?" she asked. Astonished, Laurel told her that it was their next port of call. They had booked a couple of weeks at a rustic cabana resort right on the beach at Tulum, on the Riviera Maya.

"An important meeting is taking place at Chichen Itza, near where you are staying. The Elders will be speaking about the End of Time. I have been told to tell you that you should be there. May your guides take you there safely."

Before they could say anything, the shaman got up and walked quickly over to the large bus that was waiting to take visiting day-trippers down to the town below. She disappeared into the throng of people boarding the bus.

"That was a strange experience," said Sam as they sat in the Vistadome train on their way back to Cusco, where they would board their flight for Lima the next day.

Laurel gazed out the window, her eyes admiring the scenic views of wooded canyons and the rapidly moving river below. "Yes, it was strange, and what an amazing coincidence," she replied. "How on earth did she know that we were heading for Mexico?"

That evening, they had dinner in a small local restaurant in Cusco. Laurel was having a few problems with the high altitude, or at least that was her excuse for drinking several glasses of coca wine, a local drink made of alcohol and coca leaf.

"What do you know about Chichen Itza?" asked Laurel, knowing that Sam had read many books on the Maya.

"Chichen Itza is one of the most important archaeological sites in Maya culture," he said. "Apparently, it was habitated in two different periods. The earlier buildings belong to the classic Maya period, between the 7th and 10th centuries AD, when the city was a major ceremonial centre. Arts and sciences flourished there during that period."

"Towards the end of the Classic Period," he continued, "the Maya abandoned Chichen Itza to live on the west coast of the Yucatan Peninsula for about 250 years."

Laurel was puzzled. "Why did they do that?" she asked.

Sam shook his head. "Nobody really knows why. But they did return there to live in the 10th century, constructing some of the most amazing buildings and temples, including the famous Kukulcan pyramid that sits in the middle of the ruins.

But the Toltecs were also into human sacrifice and it is said that many young women and children were hurled into the "Sacred Cenote," or Sacred Well, nearby."

She shuddered. "Let's go back to the hotel—we need to get away early in the morning.

Chapter 14

The next day, they boarded their plane for Cancun. They were looking forward to spending a week on a beach, having been so active for the past 6 months. Laurel fell asleep on the plane, still worn out by her altitude sickness.

They arrived in Cancun at about 4 pm, after stopping briefly in Miami. A local shuttle bus dropped them at the resort, and they walked in holding their backpacks.

A smiling staff member took them to their cabana, right on the beach. "This is idyllic," said Laurel. They had chosen well; the resort was small, cosy, and ideally located. After an afternoon swim, they made their way to one of the inexpensive local restaurants within walking distance of the hotel.

Laurel moaned after taking a mouthful of her Mango Salsa. "Delicious," she said. They had both ordered Carne Tacos for the main course, and these were soft, chewy, and mouth-watering. They washed the meal down with some delicious, chilled Mexican wine.

"I'm a little nervous about tomorrow," said Laurel. "I wonder what these Elders will say about the 'End of Time'?

Sam looked at her quizzically. "You, nervous? That's the last thing I would have thought you would say after everything we have experienced this year," he replied.

"This feels different," said Laurel.

"Anyway, no point in speculating," she continued. "Let's hit the sack—we have a big day ahead of us tomorrow."

Chapter 15

Leyla leaned back in the comfortable leather chair in the first-class lounge at Heathrow airport. She was glad to have made it through customs in one piece, although her husband Bahram had undergone the usual over-zealous scrutiny reserved for anybody with a Middle Eastern name or appearance. He was such a sweet, mild-mannered man, a humanitarian doctor. She shook her head in anger.

"Can I get you something?" she asked. "I'm going to have a salad. "I plan to sleep all the way on the flight and don't want to be disturbed." The lounge attendant waited patiently for their order.

"No I'm OK for now," Bahram replied, not looking forward to spending 13 hours on a plane. "I can't sleep on the flight anyway, so I'll eat a meal when we get on board."

They were both looking forward to their holiday in Mexico, a glorious 10 days in a luxury hotel resort near the Mayan ruins. They had flown into London from Tehran a week before, to do some shopping and catch up with friends and family.

Both graduates of Tehran University's elite medical school, Leyla and Bahram worked as general practitioners in a remote village about two hours from Tehran, where they felt their services were most needed. Despite their wealthy upbringing, they felt at home in the village, returning to their comfortable home in Tehran only on the weekends.

Leyla was still shaken at the recent death of a colleague, who had been detained by the country's "morals and virtues" police for being in a public place with her fiancée. They claimed she had committed suicide but everything pointed to suspicious circumstances. *What is the world coming to*? she had asked herself.

"Last call for British Airways flight to Mexico City," said the announcement. They got up and walked through the airport to the gate, boarding the plane immediately. Leyla picked up a couple of glossy magazines, then sat down and stretched her legs out on the footstool, hoping to capture a few moments of sleep before the plane took off.

Leyla and Bahram walked into their huge one-bedroom suite at the beachfront hotel. Bahram went over to the sliding doors and opened them fully, revealing a spectacular view of the Caribbean. "Fancy a drink on the terrace?" he asked Leyla with a wink.

"Yes, please," she answered. "But let me take a shower first, I'll be with you in a few minutes."

After showering, Leyla wrapped herself in the luxurious white bathrobe and joined Bahram on the terrace. "I was reading in the hotel brochure that they offer cooking lessons," said Leyla. "I was thinking of doing the Mexican cooking class, for a change. What do you think?"

"You know me, I'll try anything new," replied Bahram with a twinkle in his eye. "Let's dine at the Chef's Table tonight and I'll tell you what I expect for dinner from now on." Leyla laughed. For an Iranian, he was probably the most liberal man she had ever met. In fact, he did most of the cooking at home.

"It's a deal," she replied. "But I'm off to have a massage now in the spa, my darling. I'll see you later this afternoon."

Leyla walked down to the spa and was escorted to a secluded beachfront hut where she would enjoy an outdoor massage. As she lay there listening to the waves crash onto the beach, her mind drifted away into a peaceful slumber, as she left her worries and concerns behind.

"Madam, please turn over." Leyla woke sharply and turned onto her tummy and felt the masseuse knead her tired shoulders firmly. "This is a Sacred Mayan Massage," whispered the masseuse. "It is designed to harmonize body, mind, and spirit."

Leyla replied with a murmur, too tired to comment on what she had heard. After another 30 minutes of pure heaven, the masseuse shook Leyla gently to tell her that the massage was complete. Sleepily, she rose and put her robe back on, before preparing to walk back to her room.

"Madam, while you are in the Yucatan, you should visit the ruins here, and particularly Chichen Itza," the masseuse whispered quietly. "There is an important reason for you to go."

"Really?" Leyla replied sleepily, wanting to know more. But the masseuse had disappeared into the back room. She walked slowly back along the beach to the hotel.

That evening, as they were sitting in a huge beachside kitchen enjoying a delicious Mexican meal, Leyla mentioned the masseuse's comments to Bahram. "The masseuse this afternoon suggested we go to Chichen Itza this week. She said there was an important reason we should go. Very mysterious. What do you think?"

Bahram sipped on his drink before replying. "That could be interesting," he said. "We can't just lie on the beach the entire time we are here."

"Yes, I know," replied Leyla, although she secretly wished she could. "OK, I'll hire a car and we can see a few of the Mayan ruins in the area on the same day."

Chapter 16

If Humanity wishes to save itself from Biospheric destruction, it must return to living in Natural Time

—Pacal Votan, 603-683 AD

El Cenote Sagrado, Chichen Itza

With a slow and deliberate sense of ceremony, the elderly Mayan and his eight companions lay their colorful rugs and cushions on the ground, in preparation for a silent meditation.

They had placed 13 crystals on the ground in front of them, arranged in perfect symmetry.

The Mayan lit a candle and they all sat down, cross-legged, eyes shut in quiet contemplation. An hour went by, and they were impervious to the curious sightseers walking nearby.

Finally, they got up, picked up their rugs and crystals, and made their way over to a corner of the coffee shop next to the Cenote. They sat down, gathered some chairs around them, and waited silently.

Chapter 17

Aurelie and Jules walked down the dusty dirt road leading to the sacred Cenote. It was unbearably hot, and the sweat was dripping from their foreheads. Aurelie pushed her hair back from her face, and frowned. There was a sense of familiarity about the place, but she couldn't put her finger on it.

They finally arrived at the sacred landmark. It was a huge, circular, natural limestone well, filled with dark green, slightly murky-looking water.

Jules had been doing some research. "Apparently, the early Mayans used to conduct sacrificial ceremonies from that temple over there," said Jules, pointing to a small, crumbling stone building next to the edge of the well. "They threw semi-precious stones, metal, clay, and even humans in there as part of the ritual," he continued. "In the early 1900s, the well was dredged by an archaeological expedition and everything was taken out."

Aurelie walked over to the temple. *What a beautiful place*, she thought. The well reminded her of the grottoes she had dreamed about recently.

Suddenly, heavy drops of rain started pelting out of the sky, as thunder roared in the background. "Hurry, let's go up there," said

Jules as he grabbed Aurelie's hand and ran up towards a small row of shops sheltered under an ancient tin roof.

A few other people were already huddled in the shelter as the rain continued to pelt down. Lightning hit a tree on the other side of the well. Aurelie shivered, and then glanced around at the other people sheltering from the storm.

She saw an attractive woman, perhaps mid-forties to early fifties, smiling and holding the hand of a little blonde-haired girl of about 10. Next to them stood two smartly dressed young men in their twenties or early thirties, one of them leaning against the wooden post.

A deeply tanned, blonde woman in her thirties had her arm around a rugged young man while he filmed the storm. An elegantly dressed couple of Middle Eastern appearance were looking a bit bewildered, and holding hands. Two fair-skinned, casually dressed young women wearing smock tops and shorts were laughing and talking animatedly.

Aurelie and Jules walked along the wooden porch to the section with tables and chairs, glancing curiously at the group of people sitting in the corner. There were both men and women, all from different ethnic backgrounds. *This is odd*, she thought. *They are staring at us.*

After a few minutes, an elderly Mayan beckoned them over, asking them to sit down on the chairs they had placed out before them. Curious, they walked over and sat down. The Mayan continued to invite the others who had taken shelter to sit down in the semi-circle of chairs. Aurelie wondered if this was going to be some kind of musical performance.

Gradually, the rest of the people in the shelter joined them, and all of them sat down, glancing around at each other. Twelve chairs were filled, and one remained vacant.

Suddenly, a dark-skinned woman in her forties ran in, shaking off the rain from her hair. "It is wet out there," she laughed, as she tried to dry herself off with a sweater she had pulled out of her backpack. As there were no seats left in the place, she cautiously approached the group and sat down on the vacant chair.

The elderly Mayan smiled gently, and said with a deep, resonant voice, "Now that you are now all here, the circle is complete, and we can begin."

Chapter 18

"Welcome," he said. "You are here today because you have all chosen to play an important role in helping humanity at this critical time. There is some information that you should know that will help guide you through this great transition."

The group exchanged looks of bewilderment, but turned their attention back to the Mayan to hear what else he had to say.

He cleared his throat, and continued. "We are currently living in what is known as the 'Mayan End Times'. More than 13 centuries ago, Pacal Votan, a powerful ruler of the Mayan Empire and master of astronomy, predicted the closing of this world age cycle of 26,000 years on December 21, 2012.

"As this date approaches, humanity is experiencing a transition phase of the old world dying and a new world being reborn."

The Mayan looked at the sky, and continued.

"On that day, a rare astronomical alignment takes place between the Earth, the Sun, and the centre of the Milky Way.

"This alignment, which occurs once every 26,000 years, has been referred to as a major transformational event by many sources including the Maya, Hopi, Inca, Cherokee, Seneka, Zulus, Maoris, Hindu, Chinese, Tibetans, and many major religions.

"It can be explained in this way," he continued.

"The physical universe exists within a rhythm of expansion and contraction. It takes 26,000 years for the Earth's rotational pole to move around the ecliptic pole, a process known as the Precession of the Equinoxes. These major cycles of 26,000 years are divided into five cycles of about 5,125 years, which are in turn divided into 13 'Baktuns' or periods of about 394 years.

"We are now in the last phase of the fifth world cycle, (1618-2012AD), at the end of which the pendulum will reach its uppermost point and pause for a second before it starts to contract.

"This is the turning point of the change in world cycles. During this phase, Pacal Votan foretold that humanity would lose its sense of oneness with nature, and its connection with natural time."

He looked at the group gravely. "We know this to be true. By relying on external clocks and calendars, which are not part of nature's sense of order, humanity has forgotten its intrinsic sense of time.

"In fact," he continued, "time's cycles are within our bodies, and within Nature's seasons and cycles. This instinctual knowledge is what enables us to live synchronistically, communicate telepathically, and always be in the right place at the right time.

"Just like you have all found your way here at this particular time today."

He smiled gently.

"You are asking what this means to you as a human race.

"To answer your question, you must first accept that life is not what it appears to be. As your scientists have shown, everything in the universe is simply a field of energy, a collection of electromagnetic particles vibrating so fast that they *appear* to be solid.

"As human beings, you are immensely powerful, and intrinsically connected to nature, eachother, and the world around you. Your power lies in your ability to modify this field around you, and create your own reality based on your thoughts, emotions and feelings. Much like biological computers, processing information from the field as an ordinary computer accesses the wireless internet.

"Yet because this concept is as yet misunderstood, most of you believe that you are helpless victims of the world around you, rather than co-creators responsible for everything that happens!"

The Mayan stood up, walked over to the edge of the porch, and continued.

"At this turning point between world cycles, which may occur at any time before and after December 21, 2012, you will all have the opportunity to transform and realize your full potential.

"Prepare for this moment. This is the call for the Light Ones among you to awaken, reunite, and harmonize the Earth, bridge the gaps among continents, religions, cultures, and races for all ages, and for all time. Now is the time to expose the corrupt practices that have suppressed humanity for so long, and replace them with sustainable systems that will serve you. This is something you all decided to do long ago.

"There are three keys that will help you. Firstly, *seek the truth*, to gain an understanding of the greater meaning of life. Secondly, *meditate or pray*, to clear your auras, quieten your mind, and put you in touch with the universal intelligence within. Thirdly, *show love, compassion, and service* to others, friends and perceived enemies alike."

The Mayan continued. "More information will be revealed to you over the next few weeks about the exact nature of this transition. It will be revealed at the right time, in accordance with the laws of synchronicity. Please share these insights with each other, and as many people as you can through your circles of influence.

"Be conscious of the power of the four great challenges: *fear, reason, social convention,* and *tradition.*

"Fear may cause you to reject this alternate view and seek comfort in your familiar yet illusionary world. Reason will try to talk you out of your inner beliefs, by discrediting them through rational arguments and logic. Social pressure may try to embarrass you. Tradition will try to hold you back by filling your minds with familiar, but limiting beliefs.

"Stop handing over your power to others. Every time you give in to peer or social pressure, that is exactly what you are doing.

"Wait for the signs to come, and they will. But beware: the greatest changes during the birth of the New World shall be in the inner planes, not from the external or physical plane, which will just be outward symptoms of internal turmoil.

"So it matters not where you are in the world, and taking shelter of a material form may not protect you from the impending storm. The events of which we speak will begin to take place, so you will see the truth of our words."

The rain had stopped. A grey-haired woman with deep-set, penetrating eyes got up and picked up the crystals piled up on the table nearby, and handed one to each of the group. "Please follow me," she said. "We are going to complete this ceremony by returning these precious crystals to the Great Spirit that dwells in the Sacred Cenote.

"She is a channel to the heart of Mother Earth, to the female essence of the Unity Consciousness Grid, and we need to help her heal."

They got up and followed her down to the side of the well. "Please meditate on the crystal with loving intent, then throw it into the water," she said. They did as she asked, and eventually all the crystals had been thrown into the water.

The group gazed silently into the well. Suddenly, the surface started to clear of leaves and become more vibrant. The glow of 13 lights appeared just under the water. A wave of the most overwhelming joy and love swept over them, as if something in the well was communicating with them and sending its gratitude for the gifts it had received.

This is all anybody ever needs, Aurelie thought. She squeezed the crystal that Julia, the shaman from the Temazcal, had given her. She felt intuitively that she had experienced the presence of God.

The woman smiled at the group. "This feeling that we all experienced," she said, "is a vision of the Aquarian Age. It has only lasted a few moments, but when you are connected to the Spirit within you, it can be there permanently.

"As humans, we have spent too much time trying to find this joy through material possessions, or through others. We have been looking in the wrong place. It was always there, within your reach. Within your heart."

Chapter 19

The butler brought a tray of Margueritas to edge of the pool, where Aurelie was standing with Jules, Laurel, and Sam. They were the first guests to arrive at the luxury villa where Trish was staying on the Playa del Carmen. Trish had invited the group to dinner after their shared experience at Chichen Itza.

Aurelie took a sip of her Marguerita and sighed. "Delicious," she said. "I know, Mexicans are experts at these," said Laurel with a laugh. Sam and Jules were talking animatedly about films, so the girls decided to walk onto the beach to dip their toes into the ocean.

They had all warmed to each other immediately. It was more than just their shared experience, it was a feeling of recognition that none of them could really explain.

"Dinner is served," called out Trish as the butler opened a bottle of wine on the side table nearby. They were eating dinner at a huge outdoor dining table, on a cream stone terrace next to the beach. It was still light, but there were several flares implanted in the sand.

They sat down, and the waiter brought out several breadboards with home-baked breads and a selection of flavored butters. He poured the wine and water, then returned to the kitchen where the chef was preparing a delicious seafood meal.

Trish smiled and held up her glass. "Welcome. This is a toast to new friendships," she said, as they raised their glasses. "That was quite an experience we had last Friday," she continued.

Aurelie nodded her head. "I still can't get over the feeling I had when we threw the crystals into the well," she said. "I have never felt that way before in my entire life. It was like a huge spiritual orgasm that seemed to go on and on." The others laughed.

"I know what you mean," said Penny. "I felt as if I were in a state of bliss. It was overwhelming."

"I had a sense of déjà vu, like it was a feeling that I had forgotten about," said David. "It certainly defies logic, but then, logic has nothing to do with it."

The waiter brought a steaming dish of Seafood Parrillada to the table, along with several side dishes of vegetables.

"I saw it as a glimpse of how we could feel all the time, or had the potential to feel if we just tapped into our inner Spirit," said Laurel.

Guy frowned and looked out to the ocean. "I wonder what is going to happen, and when it will be revealed," he said. "I must be honest, I am feeling a little apprehensive."

"I agree," said Aurelie. "I think the next few months will be very interesting – and challenging – for us all. But I think that we will all be making changes to our lives after this experience."

She looked around the group.

"Big changes," she added. "We can never go back."

PART TWO

THE REALIZATION

The Warrior of Light is now waking from his dream.

He thinks: 'I do not know how to deal with this light that is making me grow.' The light, however, does not disappear. The Warrior thinks: 'Changes must be made that I do not feel like making.' The light remains, because 'feel' is a word full of traps.

Then the eyes and heart of the warrior begin to grow accustomed to the light. It no longer frightens him and he finally accepts his own legend, even if this means running risks. The Warrior has been asleep for a long time. It is only natural that he should wake up very gradually.

—Paul Coelho

Chapter 20

As greater light continues to illuminate the planetary consciousness, darkness is necessarily accentuated. Where there is light there must exist its corresponding shadow, or contrast, for in a dualistic universe one cannot exist and is meaningless without the other

—Anonymous

"The Master" poured himself a second whisky from the decanter on the polished mahogany buffet and walked out onto the spacious terrace of his Long Island home. He took a sip from his glass and gazed out at the ocean. He could see the Fire Island lighthouse flashing in the distance.

Our plans are unfolding as scheduled, he thought. *After tonight's meeting, we will have tied up every loose end. We will be unstoppable.*

The limousines started to arrive outside the front of the house. He walked back into the sitting room to greet his guests. They had all arrived at once, which made it very convenient. He wanted to get the meeting over as quickly as possible, so that he could get an early night. He was exhausted after many weeks of travel.

"Good evening gentlemen," he said quietly. "I hope your journeys here today were not too tiring. James will serve your drinks before we start the meeting."

The butler served the drinks and quickly left the room.

"Thank you for your letters," he continued. "I believe that we have the makings of a watertight strategy that will take us to our ultimate objective." He looked at the tall man standing on his right. "Barker will present a summary of the highlights for you all. I would then ask you each to set in place the finer elements of the plan."

Barker stood up and cleared his throat, then gazed around the room with a blank, almost reptilian stare. "As The Master pointed out at our last meeting, we need to intensify our strategies to counter the awakening of humanity. The Aquarian Energy is increasingly powerful, so we have fine-tuned our approach to match it.

"We need to be one step ahead of them. We need to disguise our true intentions in everything we do. Luckily, most of the population does not believe in a secret agenda and will trust what we say.

"We will start by further destabilizing the world's economy and dramatically enhancing the state of fear, despair, and hopelessness. More banks will collapse and merge, underwritten by our puppet governments. Thousands of jobs will be lost, and entire families will be thrown out of their homes through foreclosures. Food, oil and energy prices will spiral out of control.

But this will not be enough," said Barker grimly. He walked over to the powerpoint presentation set up on the far side of the wall.

He pulled up a slide that had a diagram of an electronic device.

"We need to start implanting microchips in the population to control their thoughts and actions more directly. This chip will keep their vibrations at a level where they will never ascend to the next dimension, as well as keep them within our complete control.

"We will continue to work towards a 'cashless' society and move to start implanting chips into humans for use instead of credit and cash cards. Since this move will be unpopular and take some time, we have devised some creative ways to begin the process.

"Our pharmaceutical companies have developed several new bacterial strains that could infect the population and develop into a global pandemic. We will start to release these into the population and then provide the vaccine 'solution' that will include a tiny nanochip Radio Frequency Identification tracking device. Nobody will even know it's there.

"We need to focus first on the young, many of whom are the new warrior race 'Star Children'. Pregnant mothers are another target, as this will affect their unborn child as well.

"In terms of structured population control, our European Union is already gaining control over European countries, and EU law is overriding local country laws. Our investment in terrorist cells continues to encourage dissent from those sections of the population. Further attacks will enable us to enforce even stricter security and identity controls on the population, so that every single person on the planet is accounted for. Soon, we will have them all under our control, and the battle will be won."

The group of men applauded. The Master smiled coldly. "We have been successful in creating a feeling of insignificance and powerlessness in the human population for centuries. We have convinced them that the answer to all of their needs is external, and kept their minds too busy too look within.

"There is only a small amount of time to go before we achieve our goal. But let us be vigilant. It is becoming more and more difficult to fool them.

"We are in great danger at this time, my friends. Firstly, of being exposed. Secondly, of the possibility that people will awaken to their innate power and overcome us. The Aquarian Energy is facilitating this. We must achieve complete control before this ever has a chance of happening. Good evening, gentlemen."

Chapter 21

"Tu veux un café?"[2]

Aurelie opened one eye to look at Jules. She was still exhausted after their long trip back from Cancun. Jules was getting ready to go to his 10am class. She hadn't slept well the previous night, and was still suffering from jetlag. She turned over on her stomach, and pulled the covers over her head. *"Non merci. Je vais dormir un peu. A ce soir, bisous."* [3]

Jules disappeared through the front door; she heard the sound of the door banging downstairs as he left the building. He had been acting a little strangely since they had returned from Cancun. It wasn't anything obvious, but something her intuition had picked up.

Don't read too much into it, thought Aurelie as she drifted off to sleep. Her imagination had a tendency to get carried away.

After sleeping for about an hour, she woke up suddenly, in a sweat. She had dreamed that the ocean was rising and invading a house she was living in. She wasn't afraid, but others were panicking and running around in fear. Suddenly four people she

---

[2] Do you want a coffee?
[3] No thanks. I want to sleep a little, see you tonight.

seemed to know came out of the ocean and handed her some things she would need for the next stage of her journey.

They were all tinted pale blue, as if part of the ocean. She remembered a man and a little girl who was like a daughter to her. Then they faded back into the blue mist that was surrounding them.

She sat up in bed and looked around the room, wondering what to do next. She didn't mind doing nothing at all while away on holidays. It just didn't feel right when she was back home, where she was used to the daily routine of work, more work, and sleep.

Interspersed by occasional play. So occasional that she had forgotten how.

She got up, threw on some clothes, and went downstairs to the café on the corner for her morning coffee and croissant.

"*Bonjour*," called out Louis from behind the bar. "*Vous avez pris un jour de congé?*"[4] he asked, wondering why she was there after 11 in the morning.

"*Non, j'ai quitté mon travail*,"[5] she replied abruptly. She sipped her coffee at the bar and took a bite out of a freshly baked croissant.

She wondered how many more people she would have to explain herself to.

---

4   Are you on holidays?

Back in the flat, she switched on her computer and picked up her emails. All the usual stuff, emails from friends and industry colleagues wondering what on earth had happened. She didn't want to face them. It was as if they were part of a former life that she could no longer relate to.

That night, they went out to a local restaurant. As they sat down, Aurelie noticed a man at the next table glance at them both, then look away. There was something about him she didn't like, but she couldn't put her finger on it. Did he remind her of somebody?

She shrugged her shoulders and picked up the menu, deciding to shut everything else out except her and Jules.

"How was your day?" she asked.

Tough getting back into the routine, but OK," Jules replied.

"What about you?"

"I was thinking about what to do next," she replied. "There is so much to think about. Not only work, but also what happened in Mexico. I had another strange dream about the ocean rising this morning. Not sure what it all means."

"I've been thinking about it too," said Jules. "I'm starting to feel a little dubious about what the Elders said. I mean, these end of world predictions have happened before, but we are still here!"

---

5   No, I left my job.

Aurelie thought carefully for a few minutes before replying. "The logical, lawyer brain part of me agrees with you. But my gut feeling says that this is different. I'm going to take some time while I am home to check a few of these theories out on the Internet.

I'm not going to dismiss this just because it sounds far-fetched. Most people reject new ideas because they seem so far outside their frame of reference, but it's only because they don't see the whole picture. Remember Galileo?"

Chapter 22

The next day, Aurelie got to her computer at 9am. After checking her emails, she typed the words Natural Time into Google. She remembered that Pacal Votan, the Mayan king and prophet, had said the world was not living in Natural Time.

A site about Natural Time came up. She clicked on it and began to read:

The Law of Time states that there is only one timing frequency that unifies the whole galactic order, and this is the 13:20 ratio found within the 13-moon calendar and our human bodies, 13 main joints and 20 fingers and toes. There are 13 moons every year, each 28 days long. The 13 moon 28 day calendar has been in use for over 5,500 years as a harmonic standard. This changed after the worldwide adoption of Pope Gregory XIII's 12 month calendar system (1582) and perfection of the 12 hour 60 minute mechanical clock.

Funny, that's the same date the Elder mentioned we stopped using Natural Time, thought Aurelie. She continued reading:

The presence of this clock gave rise to the idea that time lies outside our bodies and that it can be tracked by a machine, instead of by our intrinsic sense of time. By following false timing standards, we lose our trust in an inner sense of timing, and the natural ability of being at the right place at the right time.

OK, does that mean I should throw my watch away? thought Aurelie. *The whole world works on clock timing. I'm not sure how this could work,* she thought. *Maybe I can drift into my yoga class 15 minutes late and use the excuse that my inner body clock got it wrong?* Her yoga teacher would probably accept that, she thought wryly.

She continued reading:

The number 13 has developed a poor image due to its association with the 13 moons, and the 13 cycles of a woman's annual fertility cycle. However, 13 actually represents unity, the connectedness that unifies all of creation like one magical orchestra, as the 13 tones of creation.

There were 13 of us at the meeting, she remembered. *Sounds like more than a coincidence.*

In 1933, the League of Nations (original United Nations) actually voted the 13-Month Calendar as the new world standard, because of its continuity and reliability. The 13th month was to be named "Tricember." Before it was implemented, however, the Vatican created sufficient skepticism to prevent its introduction.

Aurelie stopped reading and got up to make a cup of herbal tea. As she poured the steaming hot water into the cup, she started to think about what she had read. The information seemed to back up what they were saying about not living in Natural Time. But what did it all mean? How could just changing calendars make a difference to our spiritual or mental states?

One thing comes to mind, she thought. *By using a calendar that does not reflect the true rhythms of nature, we could be viewing*

Nature itself as irrelevant. It's almost as if we are controlling her, instead of living in harmony.

She looked up another link on the Mayan calendar.

The Mayan calendar was never about time, but rather about measuring and keeping track of the flow of creation, and the meaning of every single day. The universal law "what you pay attention to you become conscious of" comes in to play here. If our daily consciousness were attuned to our intuition instead of our constantly distracting thoughts, we would always make the right choices, be in the right place at the right time.

That makes sense, she thought. *I can relate to the bit about intuition. Whenever something seems wrong, and I don't follow my gut feeling, it inevitably ends up getting me into hot water. That could be what the Elders were talking about. Aligning ourselves with the natural time of nature and our intuition. They are probably all connected anyway.*

She decided to rent a farmhouse in the country for a few weeks to get back to nature. She also wanted to get out of Paris for a while and away from her well-meaning but slightly irritating friends and colleagues. Aurelie loved the picturesque villages of the Dordogne, so she started her search in earnest.

Chapter 23

"*Cheri, j'ai envie de me casser pour une semaine ou deux. Ça te déranges?*"[6] Aurelie wasn't sure why she was even asking Jules if it bothered him that she should go away for a couple of weeks. In fact, she was sure it would probably suit him as he had exams coming up in a few weeks and needed time to study.

"*Comme tu veux,*"[7] answered Jules accommodatingly. Although she was quite fond of him, there was something not right about their relationship at the moment, so it was a good opportunity for her to get away for a few weeks.

That night, she packed her suitcase to prepare for the next day. She had booked a pretty farmhouse with wonderful rural views, and it looked idyllic. Aurelie piled a few books in her case, books she had bought years ago but never had time to read. *Funny how your priorities change when you stop working.*

Early the next morning, Aurelie set off in her car for the Dordogne. She drove out of Paris, heading for the A10 going to Bordeaux. It was going to be quite a long drive, about 5 hours,

---

6   Darling, I'd like to get away for a week or two. Do you mind?

7   Fine by me

and she was going to try to do the trip without stopping. She drove steadily, blissfully unaware that she was being followed.

Aurelie finally arrived at the farmhouse, which was located just outside Brantôme, one of the most picturesque villages in the region. She took her bags in, then drove into the small town to pick up a few provisions. She loved the tiny, quaint grocery stores and *boulangeries* in these small towns. Before leaving, she sat down for a coffee in a small coffee shop in the centre of town.

A tall man of about 45 with piercing blue eyes came out to take her order. "*Un café, s'il vous plaît,*"[8] she asked. He smiled at her, and for a moment she felt her heart jump. *Oh my god,* she thought. *That hasn't happened for a while.*

There was something really familiar about him, but she wasn't sure what. She started to ask him questions about the coffee, and how long the shop had been opened. He told her his name was Sebastien, and that he had bought the shop about a year ago after leaving his job as a business consultant in Paris.

He had turned it from a small grocery shop into a specialty coffee shop/delicatessen, serving homemade ice cream, special blends of coffee, and other local Perigord delicacies.

Aurelie paid for her coffee and left, with the lingering image of his blue eyes in her mind. She made a mental note to go back there for coffee over the next few days.

---

8   Coffee please

That evening, back in her rented farmhouse, Aurelie stretched out on the comfortable couch with a glass of wine. *It's great to get away from the rat race*, she thought to herself.

She switched on her laptop to pick up her emails and sent a quick email to Jules to see how he was. Still puzzled about the Natural Time concept, she asked him what he thought. He did not reply immediately, so she assumed he must be out.

Exhausted from the long drive, she fell asleep on the sofa.

Chapter 24

Aurelie woke early the next morning, prompted by the rays of sun coming in through the French doors of the lounge room. *Surprisingly good sleep*, she thought. *Must be the country air*.

She walked over to the kitchen, which was open-plan *Americaine* as the French put it, and switched on the kettle. She had bought some croissants the night before and put two in the oven to heat up.

She sat down on the sofa again and poured herself a steaming hot cup of coffee. *I think I'll stay on the couch all day*, she thought as she took a bite out of one of the hot croissants. *In fact, I think I'll stay here all week. This life of leisure is becoming increasingly pleasant.*

She restarted her computer and noticed that Jules had replied to her email about Natural Time. *He's keen*, she thought, considering he had exams to sit that week.

Hi Aurelie,

I found out some interesting stuff about the time theories last night. Some pretty eminent scientists appear to corroborate some of what the Elder was saying. Notably about time not being linear, multi-dimensions, and so on. One of them is that highly respected British physicist Stephen Hawking, who wrote that best-seller A Brief History of Time.

Another is theoretical physicist and author Michio Kaku, who has degrees from Harvard and UC Berkeley. He conducted a number of experiments for a BBC program that show that we all have a unique knowledge of time, "know" our past and future, have an internal body clock controlled by the pineal gland in the brain. Interesting too that in ancient times the pineal gland was also known as the "third eye," which we no longer really use. Makes sense, as we don't refer to our own body clocks any more.

Kaku has also written books on what they call "modern string field theory," which is an explanation of the Big Bang theory of how the Universe began 13.7 billion years ago. His theories on time are entwined with the whole thing. He says that the Universe undergoes continuing creation, a bit like a constantly expanding soap bubble, and that there are other soap bubbles as well. The soap bubbles are dimensions—i.e., our 3 dimensional world, plus another 8 parallel universes we are not aware of, all vibrating at different dimensional levels but as close as a millimeter away from ours.

He suggests that the universe started a bit like a guitar string that has been plucked by stretching the string under tension across the guitar. The notes it emanates then translate into matter, i.e., the 11 dimensions he talks about. He is actually quoted saying, "The Mind of God is cosmic music resonating through 11 dimensional hyperspace."

What's really exciting is that he feels that humanity is poised to shift from its 3rd-dimensional state to a higher dimension, if we can overcome our self-destructive natures.

Anyway, I'll keep you posted on anything more I find out.

Je t'embrasse[9]

Aurelie got up from the sofa and walked over to the French doors. She opened them and stepped outside into the garden.

---

[9] Love

Jules's email was challenging all her previously held views about spirituality and science. *I always thought one contradicted the other*, she thought to herself. *But in this instance, they seem to concur. About a pretty important concept as well.*

She walked down to the pool to see if it was clean. The water looked fresh and cool, so she decided to have a swim. Stripping off her clothes, she dived in and swam several laps before climbing out and grabbing a large towel that was conveniently placed on the deck chair nearby.

I could live here, she thought. *I'm going to spend the rest of the day just relaxing. What the hell, anyway, I'm not planning to start working full time again for a while.* She closed her eyes and tilted her face towards the sun.

Chapter 25

Aurelie had a vivid dream that night, in which a light being appeared to her in a huge crystal cavern. He began to speak.

"I have an important message for you.

"You are soon to make the Great Transition, but there is much preparation to be made leading up to this event. You and many others, as well as the Earth itself, will make an evolutionary leap from the present 3rd dimensional space to the 4th and 5th dimensions.

"To achieve this process, you must reach and maintain a high vibrational state. Let me explain what this means. You have already been told that your world is composed of vibrating particles that you have the innate ability to control. In fact, you create your world through your holographic interpretation of your thoughts.

"You are currently living in times that can induce a lower vibrational state, one of fear, misery, despair. Do not allow yourselves to be dragged into this illusion. Now, more than ever, you must keep your vibrations high – in other words be happy, joyful and grateful - to prepare for the transition.

"Your thoughts, emotions, choices and actions will play a role in determining your vibrations. So choose to live in peaceful surroundings, spend time in nature, keep company with supportive, loving people, and eat healthy foods.

"You will be challenged. When this happens, remember that this world is all of your own making, and you can control the outcome if you desire. Shift your focus and replace your thoughts of despair with thoughts of love and gratitude for what you have, however little.

"Do not be fooled. Remember, this is an illusionary world that you have the power to change through your thoughts and emotions. You control your individual universe, and you collectively control the world around you. Just imagine life as you would like it to be.

"Take back your power, and do this before it is too late. The new age is dawning, and you must be in a high vibrational state to make the shift from the 3rd dimension and attain this next step in your evolution – which has been your legacy since the dawn of time."

Aurelie woke suddenly, remembering every word of the dream. She immediately fired up her computer and sent an email to the group, before falling back into a deep sleep.

Chapter 26

The next day, Aurelie woke up feeling rested. Her mind drifted to the dream from the night before. *Let's see what the others think.* She switched on her computer and checked her emails, but nobody had replied.

She made herself an expresso, picked one of the brochures about the area, and started reading:

Brantôme was originally home to the Celts, who took advantage of the extensive network of caves as well as the source of underground water to set up permanent camp. In the 8th century, an order of Benedictine monks built an abbey and church, which was then rebuilt as the church of Saint-Sicaire in the 15th century. Behind the abbey is the fountain of Saint-Sicaire, which was part of the pilgrimage route because it was said to have magical effects on fertility. It is set within a group of caves gouged from the limestone cliffs, featuring carvings of the 'Last Judgement'.

This place is fascinating, so mystical, thought Aurelie. *Just the place I need to unwind for a few months.*

Aurelie decided to go into town to get a few more provisions—plus she wanted a cup of coffee and dose of Sebastian's smile to keep her going for the day.

After picking up a pain de campagne and some fresh fish for the evening, she dropped into Cafe Joly for a coffee. Sebastian came out to greet her with a huge smile. "Bonjour," she said shyly. Once she ordered a coffee, Aurelie asked him what it was like to live in the area.

Sebastian confirmed what she had thought, that the town was peaceful, crime free, and still lively in winter, which could be a problem with very touristy towns.

She asked Sebastian about the town's history as well. He told her that it was originally habitated by the Celts who were attracted to the underground spring, the river, and the ley lines. They considered these kinds of places filled with life energy, carried by the ley lines that represented the veins and arteries of the Earth.

"The Celts were very much in tune with nature and the seasons, weren't they?" asked Aurelie.

"For the Celts, time was circular rather than linear, replied Sebastian. "Their festivals were timed with the Earth's natural rhythms and seasons—such as Summer and Winter Solstices, the Equinox and so on. Women were highly honored for their fertility and creativity as the natural givers of life."

"Why did the Christians build a church here?" asked Aurelie. "Nearly all ancient Christian churches are built on ley lines," he replied. "When they converted the "Pagans," they simply built over their original sacred sites so that the transition was easier. They say that they also liked these spots because this energy, when flowing normally and in balance, can produce a feeling of calm and inner peace."

Aurelie looked at him with a smile. "I can feel that sense of peace already, and I have only been here for a couple of days!"

Sebastian looked at her intensely. "Are you planning to stay for long?" he asked.

"Yes, I think I'd like to buy a house here," she replied. "This is the most peaceful place I have been to for years."

Aurelie drove back to the farmhouse, her head spinning from what she had heard. *Amazing how this time issue keeps coming up again and again*, she thought. *Almost as if I'm meant to be here. This place is linked with Nature, her cycles and rhythms.*

Aurelie stretched out on the comfortable sofa and started up her laptop. *Let's see if anybody has replied to my email.* She saw responses from Penny, Trish and Guy. She opened the email from Penny first.

Dear Aurelie,

Interesting stuff. This whole concept of life as a 'holographic illusion' has been corroborated by several physicists trying to explain the nature of life. Alain Aspect, from the University of Paris, did an experiment in 1982 that showed that under certain circumstances subatomic particles such as electrons are able to instantly communicate with each other, irrespective of the distance between them which could range from 10 to 10 billion kilometres.

Then David Bohm from the University of London suggested that these findings indicate that *reality does not actually physically exist,* but is in fact a very sophisticated hologram – in other words, a three-dimensional photograph made with the help of a laser. Sounds fantastic – yes, but I'll explain his reasoning. To create a hologram, you shine a laser beam onto an object, then shine a second laser beam off the reflected light of the first, and the area where the two lasers combine is captured on film. When the developed film is lit up by a third laser beam, a three-dimensional image of the object appears.

The interesting thing about holograms is, unlike normal photographs, every small part of them has all the information of the whole picture. This is why Bohm suggested that the universe is a hologram, because he believed that subatomic particles are not communicating using a signal, but rather because they are part of the same thing.

Karl Pribram, a neurosurgeon from Stanford, independently found the same thing when he was researching how and where memories are stored in the brain. Many studies have shown that memories are located throughout the brain and not in any specific location. Pribam concluded from his experiments that memories are located not in the brain's neurons, but rather in patterns of impulses that crisscross the whole brain, in the same way as laser lights can crisscross a piece of film containing a holographic image.

His theories also explain why the brain can store so much information – ie about 10 billion bits in a lifetime – in such a small space, because holograms have the ability to store a huge amount of information. And when you think about how the brain works, when we are asked what comes to mind when we say a particular word, tons of associations come to mind immediately – which is another feature of the hologram.

This is theoretical physics – quantum physics – of course, but as yet is the most likely interpretation of life that has been developed.

Anyway, that's all I have found out so far. Let me know if you hear from the others.

Aurelie leaned back on the couch and thought about what Penny had written. She tapped her hand lightly. *How on earth could we just be holograms?*, she thought, as she rubbed the tops of her fingers. *And yet, according to this theory, it would be possible to **imagine** what a hand feels like.*

Still not convinced, Aurelie opened up Guy's email.

Dear Aurelie,

A friend lent me a book called 'The Field', written by investigative journalist and author Lynne McTaggart. It pulls together a huge body of scientific evidence that shows that the entire universe, including ourselves, is a giant field of energy that is controlled by human consciousness.

Obviously, many conservative scientists still resist this evidence, as it doesn't fit within their current world view. But it is so compelling that they will eventually have to come around, as others have done over the ages with so many new discoveries that changed the way we view the world.

One of the most interesting ideas was the notion of 'quantum coherence' observed by theoretical biophysicist Fritz-Albert Popp. It is the idea that the subatomic particles that make up life and the universe behave like a collection of tuning forks that resonate together in harmony, like an orchestra playing a symphony.

According to neurosurgeon Karl Pribam, our brains perceive an object by resonating with it. When we first notice something, its frequencies resonate in the brain's neurons which then communicate with another 2 sets of neurons, that construct the image we eventually see, in other words a hologram. Holograms function as a sort of lens that converts a set of frequencies into a coherent image. Pribam believed that the brain has a lens and uses the holographic principle to convert the frequencies it receives through the senses into the images we see around us.

What we can conclude from this is exactly what your dream said. As humans, we create everything around us, good and bad. Our present and future is filled with potential outcomes, that we can shape if we change our thinking. The problem is, most of us don't know about this, or don't understand it, so we continue to live at the mercy of external events. That's the challenge.

Aurelie looked out of the window at the undulating fields that surrounded the farmhouse. *Am I really imagining this? Is this all a creation of my mind? What about what other people see – why is it the same as what I see?*

She opened Trish's email.

Dear Aurelie,

I've been reading about the 'Law of Attraction', that is based on a similar theory. Esther and Jerry Hicks have written many books on the subject, and they say that we and the world around us are simply vibrating molecules that we are able to control! They believe that the human race is reactive, and not proactive in managing these vibrations, and that our lives could be so much better if we just aligned with our inner spirit, and refocused on positive thoughts and feelings.

The basis of the 'Law of Attraction' is that when you have a thought, the law of attraction will then respond to the thought. The minute we have a negative thought, and we dwell on it, it becomes a dominant thought and then the universe will present you with more of the same. They say 'how you feel about everything is how you are living'.

They suggest that to attract what we want, we must focus on that and not on what we *don't* want. The law of attraction responds to the vibration of our thoughts.

They have an interesting point about people who have unhappy lives, who never admit they could have created it themselves. Because they see themselves as life's victims, they don't focus on moving themselves out of that vibrational state and so continue the same pattern forever. Some of them can be influenced by early childhood experiences, including picking up the feelings and vibrations of their parents and then carrying these through into their lives.

Interesting, too, that Eastern religions have always said that the world we see is 'Maya', an illusion, and that although we think we are physical beings living in a physical universe this is an illusion as well.

Aurelie frowned. *It's hard to change learned patterns and beliefs,* she thought. *That's probably why we attract the same thing over and over until we change what we believe.*

Aurelie's mind was spinning. To relax, she decided to start cooking dinner, and chopped some mushrooms and garlic to make a spaghetti sauce. As the mushrooms were frying in the pan, Aurelie started to think about her decision to live in the country. What if she got bored? Would she ever be able to work again if she didn't get back into it right away?

Then she started to worry about Sebastien. What if he thought she was too forward? He must surely be married. All her habitual fears started to come back.

Suddenly, she realized what was happening. *For God's sake, stop!* she told herself. *Take deep breaths, and visualize a positive outcome, the one that you want to happen. Visualize, then let go. Trust in the process.* She took a few deep breaths. *Trust that everything that is happening is meant to happen. If it goes wrong, don't get caught up in the drama, just observe it and ask yourself why. Because you created it.*

Aurelie calmed down immediately. After dinner, she read for a while listening to La Bohème. When "Che Gelida Manina" started to play, tears started streaming down her cheeks. She was overwhelmed by the beauty of the music and the sadness she felt about the time she had spent pursuing meaningless goals.

Eventually, she decided to go to bed. She was still recovering from years of deprived sleep.

That night, Aurelie awoke suddenly and looked at the clock. It was 4.13 am. In her dream, rays of incredibly bright blue light were trying to penetrate the Earth's atmosphere, but were being blocked from coming in because of a thick layer of dense smog.

She had been blowing the smog away to allow the light to come through, and when it did, it filled everything with lightness and joy.

Chapter 27

Yasmin walked confidently into the Upper East Side brownstone where she had arranged to meet Guy and David for a drink. Glancing around the room, she saw them sitting at the end of the bar, which was glowing with hundreds of tea lights.

Guy waved as she approached them, and greeted her with a huge smile. Yasmin had experienced an instant rapport with both of the men. It was as if they were part of the same family.

As she sat down on the leather bar stool, David asked her what she wanted to drink. Looking up at the wall behind the bar, she saw a selection of 100 vodkas on display. "I'll have a vodka and tonic," she replied.

"Vodka and tonic and two watermelon martinis," said David to the barman. "Actually, make that three," said Yasmin.

Guy took a couple of chips out of the bowl in front of him. "How was your meeting with the environmentalists?" he asked Yasmin.

"It was quite an eye opener," she replied. "I had no idea who was behind these big business drives in the Amazon. That group of powerful businessmen, the Global Elite or whatever they are called, seem to have a finger in every pie on Earth," she added.

"Hmm," said Guy. "Conspiracy theorists have been talking about this group of people for a while. Powerful family banking dynasties and the financial institutions they create and control, such as the Global Bank, the Federal Reserve. I hadn't given it any credence until recently."

"Why is that?" asked Yasmin.

"I've been consulting to one of the banks for their reorganization strategy following a recent buyout of their main rival," said Guy. "I found out that the whole thing stinks of a deal between the Fed and the bank," he continued. "It all makes sense if it's true that the Fed is just a puppet for these guys, and not really independent."

Yasmin flashed back to what Mike from Global Canopy had said to her earlier in the day. He had told her that the reason why the dam project had gone through in the Amazon was most likely because large tracts of the rainforest were actually owned by the Global Bank, which had bankrolled the Brazilian government to buy them with a view to protecting it from further encroachment.

He told her that the bank had a long reputation for funding infrastructure projects that harmed the rainforest. "But surely that goes against their entire ethos?" she had asked. "Their stated policy was to eradicate poverty." Mike had nodded ruefully in agreement.

"There's Jonathan," said David, waving at a tall, attractive man who had just come into the bar. "We asked Jon to join us for dinner tonight. He's a lawyer who works with some of the top banks, so he should be able to give us a few insights."

They followed the waiter to a table for four at the back of the room. As the waiter took their orders, Jonathan turned to Yasmin with a smirk. "I hear you guys met at a spiritual gathering in Cancun?" he asked.

"That's right," Yasmin replied wearily, irritated by his tone. "They were trying to warn us about an impending change in the world as we know it. They told us we were going to play a role in exposing corrupt practices, as well as set up better structures, so that we can shift to the next phase."

"What kinds of corrupt practices?" asked Jonathan.

"I was environmental advisor to the Brazilian government until recently," said Yasmin. "I witnessed first hand the corruption of the multinationals, in collusion with the Global Bank and the government—all controlled by members of the group they call the Global Elite, otherwise known as the 'Illuminati.' The rainforest continues to be exploited, at the expense of humankind's future survival. Sadly, I couldn't do anything about it when I was working there, and it's even less likely now."

"I've been amazed at just how much the Global Elite actually controls," added Guy. "Look at the owners and investors of

Google, Facebook, and UTube. They use the media to manipulate us into agreeing to just about everything, including going to war, which is a classic money-spinner for them."

Jonathan laughed. "For intelligent people, you are starting to sound like conspiracy theorists. Why on earth would any group of people want to control us? If they really did, why not just use military force? Why bother going to all this trouble to get our consensus?"

"History has shown that oppressive systems always get overthrown," said David. "Plus, creativity is completely stifled when people don't feel a relative sense of freedom. As a result, they tend not to be as productive, which affects the overall profitability of any company. It's all about money."

"There's also the fact that an empowered population is quite difficult to manipulate and control," added Guy.

"Come on," said Jon, "it's just business, it's the way the world has always operated. We have all made money out of this system—it's the reason why we enjoy the lifestyle we have today. Why change it? Hey, guys, wake up to reality."

Guy looked at Jonathan with a frown. "This is reality," he replied. "Why wouldn't a group of powerful people want to control the world? When people have power, they get greedy and just want more. I saw how the J.P Irving deal happened, and I can tell you, it was a carefully orchestrated plan that made a few people richer and a lot of people poorer."

"It's not just the big boys causing the problem," added David. "Fund managers and their clients don't realize that by investing in commodity, food and oil stocks they are exacerbating the global crisis."

"Hey, if you guys want to turn into bleeding-heart liberals then go ahead," replied Jon with an expressionless stare. "At the end of the day, it's all about choice. I believe in survival of the fittest—it's what has made us what we are today. I want to know that my financial future is secure with the investments I make. If a few people get hurt along the way, then so be it."

"What if you knew that by hurting others you were actually hurting yourself in some way?" asked Yasmin. "I think that the signs all around us point to the fact that we aren't getting away with it anymore. If it's true that we are all connected, then every action we take is somehow going to come back to us, sooner or later."

"Well, there are still some very rich people around the world, and every day they are getting richer," replied Jon. "I doubt that many of them made their fortunes by living in absolute integrity. Nothing seems to be happening to them," he added.

"Not yet," said Yasmin. "But it's just a matter of time."

Chapter 28

The next morning, Yasmin left for Rio. She was exhausted and slept most of the way, relishing the moment that she would be back in her own bed.

Her friend Manuela was there at the airport to greet her. As they set off on the 2- hour journey to the apartment they shared in Buzios, Manuela asked her about the trip.

"It was life-changing experience," she said to her friend. "I had a particularly interesting time in Cancun. I'll tell you about it over dinner. How is preparation for the Samba Parade going?" Manuela ran one of Rio's top samba schools, which had won first prize at the prestigious Samba Parade for the last five years.

"Pretty well," replied Manuela. "Can I rely on your creative input again this year? I need a show-stopping theme and so far my mind is a blank."

"Delighted," said Yasmin. She loved the annual Samba competition, but had never had much time in the past to get involved. Now that she wasn't working, she could spend more time helping Manuela put the theme together. She closed her eyes and started to doze.

Yasmin woke up suddenly as the car pulled in front of their condominium complex in Buzios. They didn't see the car drive off, nor did they know that their apartment had been fitted with the latest surveillance equipment.

Manuela typed in the code to open the security gate, and they drove into the parking garage and into Manuela's stall.

"I'm exhausted," said Yasmin as they took her luggage into the house. "I think I'll take a nap. We can go into Buzios for a meal later this evening if you want."

"Sounds good," replied Manuela as she sat down on the comfortable sofa. I'll see you in a couple of hours.

Yasmin collapsed on her bed and fell into a deep sleep. After a few hours, she woke up with the memory of a deep, resonant sound, which seemed to be emanating from the centre of the Universe. She fell back to sleep, and dreamed of being transported to a crystal cave where a light being spoke to her.

"I have the second message for you and your tribe.

"Just as the universe is composed of vibrating particles, sacred sound is the basis of all creation. Every cell, every particle in your bodies is a sound resonator, that can be altered, strengthened or balanced through the use of sacred sound.

"So, to help you to reach the next level of evolution, waves of vibrational sounds are cascading through the universe to assist with your ascension. All of you will increase your vibrations, although this will have a twofold effect: some of you will experience distress, while others will ascend in consciousness.

"To ensure that you among those who ascend, it is important to see through the illusion of the present world, and not be attached to its conflict and disharmony. You must acknowledge your role as co-creator of your existence and stop blaming others for you misfortune or unhappiness.

"These waves of vibrational sounds will be activating new strands of your DNA, that will alter your brain in ways you never thought possible. You will grain increased mental and spiritual abilities, and connect to other dimensions and vibrations. Everything will appear lighter and more luminous, and you may feel as if you are living in a dream.

"The upcoming transition will take the form of billions of strings of energy elevating their octaves, and resonating together to create a balanced symphony of perfect change. The wave of music will resound through all the galaxies and create a joyous event of evolutionary transformation!"

Yasmin woke up suddenly, and wondered if she was still dreaming. After a few minutes, she got up and walked out into the lounge room, where she found Manuela asleep on the sofa.

She picked up her laptop and tiptoed out onto the balcony, where she settled down on one of the reclining chairs, before switching on her computer. She wrote down everything she remembered about the dream and sent it out to the group, excited that she had received the second message about the transition.

Her inbox had about 75 emails, and she flicked through them quickly to find the most urgent. There were several emails from former colleagues and work acquaintances wanting to know what her plans were. She ignored them. A couple of head-hunters she knew had also been in touch.

Then she noticed an email from Jules, sharing his research on time theories. Her eyes scanned down the page, then stopped at his comments about the origins of the universe. She read, then re-read the paragraph: "Physicist and author Michio Kaku suggests that the universe started a bit like a guitar string that has been plucked by stretching the string under tension across the guitar. The notes then translate into matter…the mind of God is cosmic music resonating through 11 dimensional hyperspace."

That's odd, she thought. *It sounds a bit like the dream I just had.*

Manuela called out to her, jolting her out of her reverie. "Feel any better?" she asked.

"Much better, thanks," replied Yasmin. She logged out and switched off her computer. "Let's hit the town. I'm starving!"

After showering and changing, Yasmin and Manuela walked out of their condominium, and within 15 minutes were walking along the Rua Das Pedras in downtown Buzios. They decided to have a drink in one of the oceanfront bars before dinner.

"Shall we order two Passion Fruit Caipirinhas?" asked Manuela with a smile, knowing what Yasmin would reply. Yasmin was always one to have a good time, even when she was exhausted.

The waiter took their order, and they relaxed in the large, comfortable lounge chairs facing the ocean. Yasmin glanced around the bar, and suddenly saw her old friend Marco sitting in the corner. "Marco," she called out. He stood up and went over to them with a broad smile.

"How are you darling?" said Marco as he put his arms around her and gave her a kiss on both cheeks.

"I've just returned from New York and Cancun, and have tons to tell you. Why don't you join Manuela and I for dinner tonight?" Marco was only too happy to agree, as he had not seen Yasmin for weeks. She had been spending a lot of time at work recently and he had been busy as well. Marco was a professional violinist in the Rio de Janeiro Opera House Orchestra, and had studied at the Federal University of Rio de Janeiro with Yasmin over 20 years ago.

They walked through the small, well-hidden door that led them to one of Yasmin's favorite local restaurants. The smiling waitress led them to a table facing the ocean, and took their orders of fresh, grilled fish, hot chips, and baked vegetables.

During dinner, Yasmin filled Marco and Manuela in on her experiences in Cancun and New York. She asked Marco what he thought about her dream, and the concept of music and its connection with the universe.

Marco looked thoughtfully at Yasmin before he replied. "They say that music, like Nature, is made up of patterns connected in an orderly and harmonious way, and that these patterns hold the universe together. Researchers have identified a 'divine proportion' in music that is found everywhere in the natural world," he continued.

"Do you mean like sacred geometry?" asked Manuela.

"Yes," replied Marco. "It is the phi, the proportion that ancient civilizations believed had a particular vibrational quality that provides incredible powers of communication. Many churches were designed using the sacred geometry, and praying within these buildings is believed to amplify a person's resonance with the higher realms. This formula also works with the universal concept of beauty. Experiments have shown that groups of people shown pictures of different faces tend to choose the ones whose features conform to the 'phi' ratio. We seem to resonate naturally with these proportional ratios."

"That's funny…I got an email this morning from one of the people I met in Cancun," said Yasmin. "He says that a respected scientist thinks that the universe was created with sound, a bit like a guitar string that was plucked then resonated through matter."

"An interesting theory," replied Marco. "Have you ever noticed the way that people respond to beautiful music? It creates a really powerful response. It can change moods, make people cry, trigger memories, make you happy or sad. It helps us resonate to our true natures, restores the harmony and balance to our beings."

"I have heard that Shamans 'sing' disharmony and disease out of people's bodies," said Manuela.

"It doesn't surprise me," replied Marco. "Have you heard of the 'Mozart Effect'? It was first written about in a 1993 paper in Nature magazine when a U.S. neuroscientist showed that college students who listened to Mozart for 10 minutes performed better on a spatial reasoning test than students who listened to New Age music or nothing at all. Since then, scientists have shown a number of positive effects such as reduced seizures in epileptics, improvements in autism and Parkinson's disease, and better learning and memory."

"How does it work?" asked Manuela.

"One of the studies showed that the particular rhythmic qualities of Mozart's music are the same as some of the rhythmic cycles occurring in human brains," replied Marco. "But it must be more widespread than that, as even plants have been found to grow better to classical music!"

"Do you think that the wrong music could have a negative effect on us?" asked Yasmin.

"Possibly," replied Marco. "Plato once said, 'In order to take the spiritual temperature of an individual or society, one must mark the music.' I have often wondered whether the mess our society is in today is linked with the largely dissonant music we listen to. Most people spend their entire lives with an iPod glued to their ears. Who knows what effect that could be having?"

After dinner, Marco walked Yasmin and Manuela back to their apartment. Yasmin felt very light-headed, a combination of fatigue and restlessness. Her mind was spinning from the recent events, as well as what they had talked about that evening. She fell asleep the minute her head hit the pillow, and slept soundly until 11 am the next morning.

Chapter 29

Yasmin woke up and walked out of her bedroom to the living area. Then she went out onto her terrace and looked over the ocean.

It was a beautiful day.

She walked back inside and switched on the kettle to make some coffee.

As she poured coffee into a cup, her mind drifted to her work situation, and whether she should apply for a job at one of the environmental agencies in Rio. *I don't want to go back. Not now, anyway.*

Instead, she decided to flesh out some ideas for the theme of the Samba festival, so that she could discuss them with Manuela that evening.

She took her cup of coffee out to the terrace, and sat down on the sun lounge. She started to write down some thoughts in her notebook.

Music, sacred music. Universe created by sound. Are we made of matter vibrating to sound? Or created by sound? Her mind continued to turn over and over. She was excited, yet very confused by her dream and what Marco had told her.

She stretched her legs out on the lounge, and gazed out at the ocean. *There has to be a way to use the "phi" principle in the song we create for the Samba competition*, she thought to herself. *The theme could be "phi" as well, harmony and sacred geometry. What about costumes designed with the "phi" principle, a new dance based on "phi," the use of natural fibres? Mozart effect?*

Yasmin started to write her ideas down in her notebook. The ideas were flowing, as if they couldn't stop. By lunchtime she had mapped out the entire concept for the Samba dance. She had even extended it to a new idea, involving setting up a social enterprise based on music creation.

She went into the kitchen to make some lunch, and decided to have a swim in the pool. Even though it was the middle of winter, Buzios enjoyed a year-round summer cooled by sea breezes.

I'm enjoying this, she thought to herself. After her swim, she checked her mail and saw a message from Aurelie regarding her dream.

Hi Yasmin,

I can understand the concept of sound being the source of creation, and that particles are sound resonators. A friend of mine here who is a musicologist lent me a few books on the subject, including 'The Cosmic Octave' by Swiss scientist Hans Cousto.

Did you know that colour and sound don't really exist? This was new to me as well. Apparently, both perception and hearing start as a vibrational frequency that is then transformed into electronic signals sent to the brain.

When we hear a sound, we are perceiving a combination of frequencies that travel from the outer ear, and are amplified between 150-200 times by the time they reach the inner ear. An organ made up of very fine hairs, known as the Organ of Corti, transforms the sound into neural signals as its cilia vibrate.

Similarly, our vision also perceives vibrating frequencies, which are then transformed and sent to the brain. We perceive frequencies ranging from 375 trillion hertz for the colour red, to 750 trillion hertz for the colour blue, with all the other colours vibrating at frequencies somewhere inbetween. As a result, we reverberate and resonate with every sound we hear.

Cousto says that DNA-RNA chains are in a state of 'harmonious resonance' to the octave tones of the earth's rotation.

This information is all leading to something – I can just feel it. We should plan to get together again when all the messages have come through to see where they are taking us. In the meantime, keep well,

Aurelie

Yasmin stood up and walked over to the window. *The picture is starting to emerge*, she thought. *It still has a few missing elements – but it is getting there.*

She returned to her notebook and started to put together her presentation.

Manuela returned from work at 7:45 that evening. Yasmin greeted her at the door with a smile. "I think I've cracked this year's theme," she said.

"So quickly?" asked Manuela.

"It just seemed to flow out of me. Can't really explain it," Yasmin replied. "Anyway, I'm making pasta for us. Take a shower and I'll show you what I have after dinner."

They ate dinner on the terrace, where Yasmin had set up the table. "It's wonderful to have the time to do this," she said.

"Agree," said Manuela. "By this time, we are usually both comatose in front of the TV. I think you should stay at home for a while," she added with a smile.

After dinner, Yasmin set her computer up in the living room. "I thought I would present this to you as if you were presenting it to your committee," she said as she started to run through the slides on her computer. Manuela sat up listened attentively.

"As history tells us, Samba's origins are linked with the Afro-Brazilian Candomble religion practiced by the refugees who fled from Bahai to Rio in the early 20th century.

"The original dance represented a form of worship, an invocation of a personal orixa (god). In the 1920s, the music and dance became a sensation in Paris, going on to achieve international acclaim.

"This year, we will celebrate the origins of Samba, in all its sacred traditions. As part of this, we will rejoice in the perfection of our beautiful Earth, mirroring the pure harmony of her incredible design.

"We will create a dance routine that reflects the natural rhythms of nature. We will create a song that resonates with the sacred sounds of the universe. We will wear costumes that celebrate nature and her majesty.

"This year, our theme will be Samba Sagrado."

Manuela applauded. "It's wonderful," she said, I can see it already."

"I've thought of something else, out of all of this," said Yasmin.

"I want to set up a music company that encourages artists to compose 'hip' and contemporary music using the principles of sacred music. I will get backing from social entrepreneurs, and my colleagues in the Green movement, to start it here, then move it worldwide. I truly believe that if we change what we listen to, we will change the way we think and start to heal our society."

"Great idea," said Manuela.

"It's time to take back control," replied Yasmin. "Not a moment too soon.'

As she said that, the woman who was monitoring her apartment picked up the phone and rang Long Island.

Chapter 30

"Please return to your seats and fasten your seat belts," said the captain over the loudspeaker. "We are landing in London in 20 minutes. Unfortunately, the sky is overcast and they are predicting rain."

Penny shook her head with disbelief. It was almost the end of June and the weather was still terrible. *Global warming is no longer a possibility*, she thought to herself. *It is now a reality.*

The plane skidded slightly as it landed on the runway at Gatwick Airport. Penny turned to Marianne, who was lying back in the seat with her eyes shut. "It was nice of you to invite Laurel and Sam to stay," she said.

Marianne yawned, then replied lazily, "I have plenty of room, as you know. It's only for a week or two anyway, and part of that time they will be outside London."

Laurel and Sam were spending a few weeks in England to visit a couple of sustainable communities in the Southwest. Sam was going to film the area documentary that Laurel was making on permaculture and sustainable lifestyles.

They saw them in the baggage collection area, looking slightly bedraggled. That was how Penny's brain felt, after everything they had experienced.

Finally, the baggage belt started and the luggage began to emerge. After a few minutes, their bags appeared, surprisingly close together. Penny and Marianne picked them up and stacked them onto a large trolley. They wheeled it over to Laurel and Sam, who were still waiting for theirs. "I've booked a minicab to take us straight home," said Marianne. Penny thanked her silently for being so efficient.

Before long, they were all piled into a cab heading for Southwest London, unaware that a car was following them from the airport. Marianne lived in one of those modern developments along the river. It was a three-bedroom apartment on the 4th floor, with a terrace overlooking the water.

"This is really nice," said Lauren as Marianne showed her their room. "I'm going to take a shower, if you don't mind." Sam nodded in agreement.

"Take your time," answered Marianne. "Let's meet out on the terrace in about an hour for a drink. Because the weather has cleared up, I thought we could have a light lunch at the Italian downstairs, then chill out this afternoon for a few hours. If you are up for it, we can take you to Southbank or into Soho tonight. It promises to be an unusually warm evening."

Penny and Marianne went to shower and change as well. They were ready before the others, so Marianne opened a chilled bottle of rosé and poured Penny a glass.

"What's with those two?" Penny whispered to her friend. "Seems odd that they sleep in the same bed but aren't together. They have been traveling together for over six months as well."

Marianne laughed. "I have no idea," she replied. "I guess it's not impossible for men and women to have platonic relationships. I gather they've known each other since they were little. A bit like brother and sister." She looked closely at her friend. "Why do you ask? Does it have anything to do with Sam?" she teased.

"Of course not," said Penny quickly. "I'm just curious, that's all." But she did feel very attracted to Sam, and wasn't sure if she would be treading on Laurel's toes if she did anything about it.

Laurel and Sam finally emerged from their bedroom, looking fresh and relaxed. They all went downstairs and were seated at an outdoor table near the river. After two pizzas and a salad, the conversation turned to their experience in Mexico.

"I saw the Dalai Lama in London recently, and his entire talk was about the fact that we are all connected," said Penny. "The Elders seemed to corroborate what he has always been saying. I've never been sure of what it all means, I must admit."

"What I'm not sure about is how 2012 fits into the frame," said Sam. "I'd like to spend some time researching it this afternoon."

He winked at Penny. "Care to join me? Think I could use some of your analytical skills."

Laurel looked at him with a smile. She knew that Sam was attracted to Penny, and was hoping that they would get together during their stay.

"I'm off to meet up with this woman who is an expert on sustainable lifestyles this afternoon," she said.

"Sounds interesting," said Marianne. "Mind if I tag along?"

Chapter 31

After lunch, they returned to the apartment. It had turned out to be a beautiful, sunny day, so Penny set her laptop up on the terrace, while Laurel and Marianne got ready to go out. "See you later," they called out as they shut the apartment door.

Sam walked into the kitchen and put on the kettle. "Tea?" he asked. "Yes, please," replied Penny as she stretched out on the lounge chair.

He brought a large pot of tea and two cups out to the terrace. "I'll get started if you want to get some beauty sleep," he said with a smile. "Not that you need it, of course."

Penny blushed as she smiled back at him. *Gorgeous brown eyes*, she thought. *I need to stop doing this until I sort out my marriage. But it's just so nice to feel appreciated for a change.*

Sam typed in the words 2012 Mayan calendar into the search engine. Several sites came up. He clicked on one and scanned the content briefly.

"Here's something about the Mayan calendar," he said, and he started to read from the site:

The Mayan calendar is a method of timekeeping in cycles and is one of the most accurate systems every known. The Mayans devised several calendars, but the ones most frequently referred to are the 260-day Tzolkin, the 360-day TUN, and the 365-day Haab. They all synchronise together and have distinctive purposes.

The Tzolkin calendar is the daily astrological calendar, featuring 13 intentions and 20 aspects of creation. In the Mayan view, the universe resonates with the energies of the calendar and every person knew why they had been born, as they identified with the message of the day. The TUN is the prophetic calendar, predicting cycles over a vast period of time, while the Haab is the more practical agricultural calendar linked with the sun and the seasons.

"How do we know they are accurate?" asked Penny.

"Archaeologists consider the ancient Mayans to have been extremely advanced in the sciences of mathematics and astronomy," Sam replied. "Apparently all of the astronomical dates and events they predicted in their calendars have turned out to be absolutely correct."

He continued reading from the page:

The Maya divided the 26,000-year period it takes for the rotational pole of the Earth to move around the Ecliptic pole, known as the Precession of the Equinoxes, into five cycles of about 5,125 years. These 5,125-year cycles, also known as the "Long Count" are in turn divided into 13 "Baktuns," or periods of about 394 years each.

"This is interesting," said Sam as his eyes scanned down the page. "According to this Mayan researcher, John Major Jenkins, the current 13-Baktun cycle, which started on the 13th August 3113 BC, is the 5th and final cycle in this Precession of the Equinoxes. We are living in the 13th, or last period of that cycle, which started in 1,618 AD and is scheduled to end on the 21st

133

December 2012. It is known both as the triumph of materialism and the transformation of matter. It this is all true, we really are at the end of an era!!"

"What does it all mean?" asked Penny.

"From an astronomical viewpoint, a unique alignment takes place on December 21, 2012, that happens only every 26,000 years. The winter solstice sun will align with the centre of the Milky Way, and this is a road into the exact centre of the galaxy.

At the same time, the Earth completes a 'wobble' around its axis, coinciding with a reversal of the Earth's magnetic poles. According to this source, it will provide a gateway to the next dimension, an evolutionary leap to the next stage in our development."

Penny looked at Sam dubiously. "Any scientific backup for that?"

Sam did another search on geomagnetic reversal of the Earth, and came up with a 2002 article on The Observer newspaper's website, commenting on a paper that had been published in the scientific journal Nature by Dr. Gauthier Hulot of the Institut de Physique du Globe de Paris.

"According to this article," he said, "the Earth's magnetic field is getting weaker, and is disappearing most alarmingly near the poles, a clear sign that a flip may soon take place. Geological surveys of the mid-Atlantic ridge show that this has occurred many times before, approximately every 13,000 years, and in the past has caused widespread earthquake activity and flooding."

"I'm still not absolutely sure what it all means," said Penny. "Is there anything more about the evolutionary leap?"

Sam did another search. "There's a scientific theory to all this by an astrophysicist, Dr Paul La Violette," he said. "He claims that the core of the Milky Way galaxy is a massive object that explodes periodically, and that this happens every 26,000 years with the possibility of a 13,000-year recurrence. When it does, it sends out a 'galactic superwave' of cosmic rays. He apparently found evidence in the ice core that the last superwave ended the ice age almost 13,000 years ago. That's also apparently when Noah's Flood was supposed to have taken place."

Sam continued reading. "The cosmic gamma rays produce high-energy electrons that become trapped by the Earth's magnetic field, forming powerful energy radiation belts. They could cause a global communications and electronic blackout by permanently damaging the electronic components of communication satellites, as well as our household appliances and cars. The cosmic dust that the superwave transports could seriously affect the Earth's climate, possibly triggering a new ice age."

Sam looked over at Penny. "What's interesting is that scientists picked up a gamma ray burst right after the 2005 tsunami. It emitted more energy in a tenth of a second than the Sun emits in 100,000 years. Dr. La Violette says that the superwave was preceded by a strong gravity wave that could induce substantial tidal forces on the Earth."

"It all sounds a bit grim," said Penny. "I really don't like hearing about disaster predictions, you know. When have we ever known any of them to be true?"

Sam nodded. "I agree with you. But some of the science is compelling. Maybe something else is going to happen that the Mayans were predicting. Something positive, perhaps?"

Penny smiled. "You are the ultimate optimist," she said. "Find something positive in all this and then let's open a bottle of wine."

"Deal," replied Sam, as he did another search on the Internet.

"Listen to this," he said. "Jenkins says that this high-frequency radiation striking the Earth can result in a transformative effect on human consciousness, and that is has done so in the past. He claims that the Milky Way alignment in 2012 will open a channel for this radiation to open our third eye and shift us to a higher level of being."

"Funny," said Penny, "my yoga teacher has been telling us that our DNA is being activated by waves of universal energy, as if we are all walking antennas. I always thought she was bonkers, actually. But I have been feeling very drained lately, as if something is going on. Supposing it is all true—do we need to prepare for it in any way?"

Sam read further down the article. "According to a geologist named Gregg Braden, to adapt to this Earth magnetic shift we have to match our resonant frequency to that of the Earth. Negative emotions block the process, but we can transcend those with the vibration of unconditional love. This can be more easily achieved near places with a low magnetic field, such as many sacred sites."

Penny closed her eyes for a moment. "Wow, this is a lot of information," she said. "Part of me wants to just dismiss it all because it sounds pretty far-fetched. But another part of me is starting to wonder..."

"Let's wrap up for the day," replied Sam. "Glass of wine?"

Chapter 32

Laurel and Marianne returned from their meetings later that afternoon. They arrived to find Sam and Penny lying asleep on the large deck chair outside on the terrace, an empty bottle of wine beside them.

"Wakey wakey," said Marianne as they walked out onto the terrace. "You guys look like you have had a productive afternoon," she said with a smile.

Penny opened her eyes slowly and smiled. "You would be surprised," she said. "We have solved the secrets of the universe in a couple of hours. But you'll have to wait until dinner to hear the grand revelation," she added playfully.

Laurel walked onto the terrace with a tall glass of cold water in her hand.

"We met a fascinating guy today," she said. "A real expert on sustainability. I will definitely interview him for my show."

"He's joining us for dinner tonight," she continued. "Apparently he's a bit of an expert on 2012 as well. Could be an interesting conversation."

Sam got up and stretched his arms out. "I feel so much better after that catnap," he said. I'm going to freshen up before we go out. See you shortly."

After Sam closed the door of his bedroom, Marianne turned to Penny with a smile. "Making progress, I see," she said.

"Nothing happened," replied Penny indignantly. *Well not yet, anyway.*

They decided to eat at Marianne's favorite restaurant on the Southbank in the Oxo Tower. As they took the lift up to the top floor, Sam glanced over at Penny appreciatively. He had really enjoyed spending time with her that afternoon.

They arrived at the 8th floor and turned right to go to the Brasserie. After announcing their arrival to the hostess, they walked straight down the hallway to the bar, where they were going to meet John Amos, the sustainability expert Laurel and Marianne had met that afternoon.

He was already there, with what looked like a vodka and coke in his hands. He smiled and jumped up, kissing Laurel and Marianne on the cheek. He shook Sam's hand and kissed Penny on the cheek after they had been introduced.

Sam went to the bar to order the drinks, while the girls sat down around the table.

"Penny and Sam have been investigating 2012 all afternoon," said Laurel. "I'm sure they have tons of questions to ask you. How long have you been researching the subject?"

"For about 5 years," replied John. "I first became interested in 2012 when I went to Mexico and read about the Mayan calendar. At first, I thought it just another myth. But upon further research, I discovered that the date, or dates around the period, is actually mentioned in a number of world religions. I started to take more notice of it at that point."

"What do you mean, 'other religions'?" said Marianne. "Do you mean Eastern religions?"

"Eastern, Western, American Indians, Zulus, Maoris, Hindu, Kabbalists, Chinese, you name it," he replied. "They all refer to a similar event occurring in the early part of this century.

"For example, the Hindu talk about powerful spiritual energies coming from the centre of the universe that will enlighten humanity, leading to a Golden Age in 2012. They also warn against negative thinking that can block this process. The Maoris talk about a Ka Hinga te Arai, a dissolving of the veil or merging of the physical and spiritual planes in 2012. The old testament in the Bible talks about a period of tribulation culminating in a Golden Age when an enlightened humanity will enter the

Kingdom of Heaven. These all sound like myths, but they have very many things in common."

Sam returned to the table holding a tray of drinks. "I'm looking forward to talking more about 2012," he said to John with a broad smile. "I have lots of questions about what we read on the Internet this afternoon."

"The Internet has tons of information, much of it contradictory," laughed John. "I've spent quite a few years trying to sort out what I think is fact or fiction. I have a library of about 10 books on the subject as well. I hope I can clarify a few points for you."

The conversation shifted to sustainable lifestyles, and the group continued talking for a while as they nibbled on peanuts and chips. The waitress from the restaurant advised them that their table was ready, so they followed her into the dining area. She took them out to the terrace, which had panoramic views of the river and the city of London.

"We are so spoiled," exclaimed Laurel. "This is absolutely lovely. What a great city you live in," she added.

"Put it this way," replied Marianne, "you've come at the right time of the year. In the winter we just stay indoors, or go drinking to the pub, and spend most of our time shivering in front of fires or heaters!"

They ordered a bottle of wine and some delicious-sounding entrees and mains, and then the subject moved inevitably back to

2012. "So what's your view on the Mayan calendar?" Sam asked John.

"I'm particularly fascinated by the Kukulcan pyramid at Chichen Itza, and the theories surrounding it," replied John. "Kukulcan is the Maya name for Quetzalcoatl, the plumed serpent and was a Caucasian god figure with blue eyes. He left in 1000 AD, promising to return.

"The pyramid was designed so that every year on the Spring Equinox, the afternoon sun's rays create a shadow on the pyramid that looks like a huge serpent coming down from the sky," John continued. "According to a 2012 Mayan expert named John Major Jenkins, this moving snake is an annual reminder of a conjunction of the zenith Sun with the Pleiades star cluster over Chichen Itza. This conjunction is an event that will only occur during a 72-year time window, from 1976 to 2048, and right in the middle of this time window is the year 2012, when the 13-Baktun cycle ends."

"How could they predict that so long ago?" asked Penny.

"Good question," John replied. "It defies explanation, but it certainly points to something they were trying to tell us. It's almost as if they were warning us of an important event that was yet to transpire. There is another theory, linking the process of the Sun to our body's chakras."

Sam looked at him blankly.

"The chakras are the body's energy centres. Let me explain how it works. Every year, the sun travels 182 days to the North and 182 days to the South, in what they call the "Cycle of the Solstices." At the midpoint in this cycle, there are the East and West cycles called the Equinoxes. On the Equinox, i.e., March and September 21st each year, the sun crosses at a central point of all the four seasons, making an exact 90-degree angle on top of the pyramid. This shadow contains seven triangles, and it apparently represents the awakening of the seven chakra centres of our bodies."

"How do they suggest that may happen?" asked Marianne.

"It has already been established that our seven chakras correlate to the position of glands in the endrocrine system of the body, and also appear to have similar biological functions," John continued. "For example, the pineal gland behind our foreheads, or the sixth chakra/third eye in the chakra system, is like a vestigial eye that controls hormone production according to the light it receives through the eyes.

"The pineal gland produces a number of hallucinogenic hormones, including DMT, referred to as the 'Spirit molecule' in certain circumstances. Harvard psychiatrist John Mack determined that DMT was produced in birth, death, near-death experiences and 'UFO' close encounters."

John looked over the river to the imposing façade of St. Paul's Cathedral. "One of the theories is that a sudden change in the

Earth's geomagnetic field—for example, caused by a major solar storm—could trigger a DMT-induced leap in consciousness for all humanity. This would result in a mass increase in psychic abilities, such as telepathy and clairvoyance. People may start to see beings in other dimensions. It has been likened to the awakening of the kundalini, the 'fire snake' in the base chakra, causing it to rise up the spines of humans, creating 'enlightenment'."

Sam and Penny looked at each other.

"What you are saying corresponds with the research we did this afternoon," said Sam. "This is sounding more and more like some kind of accelerating evolutionary path spanning 26,000 years."

"It has spanned more than 26,000 years—that is just one of the periods linked with the Precession of the Equinoxes," replied John. "A calendar that was found at Coba, one of the Mayan ruins, depicts an evolutionary path that started 16.4 billion years ago when we were at the cellular stage. Darwin's theory of natural selection never explained the many evolutionary jumps the human species has experienced, nor the extraordinary exponential growth we have seen over the past few years."

"That's true," said Penny. "We have made more progress in the past 20 years than in the hundreds of years before that."

"The Mayans mapped the whole process," continued John. "Since 1999, we have been achieving in one year what we previously achieved in 20 years. Apparently from 2011, we will achieve in one day what we are currently achieving in one year. It will be like being on a roller coaster!"

After dinner, they returned to the apartment, sobered by what they had heard. They did not see the man stalking them from a distance, talking to someone on his mobile phone.

Chapter 33

Laurel flew back to Sydney a week later, while Sam decided to stay on for a few days under the pretext of getting some more footage of the sustainable community in Somerset.

"See you in Sydney," said Laurel, as she walked through the departure gates. "Don't forget to get the footage," she added with a wink, knowing the real reason that he had decided to extend his stay.

The night before Sam was due to leave, Penny and Sam decided to go for a walk along the river. They walked past a riverside pub and decided to have a drink. After a couple of beers, Penny started to feel decidedly tipsy.

"Don't go," she said quietly, as she took Sam's hand in hers. "I'm going to miss you."

Sam stroked her hand gently. "I have to go to finish the program with Laurel. But I'll come straight back, don't worry. There's plenty of work for cameramen in London."

"I'll be counting on it," said Penny tearfully. She wiped her hand over her eyes and blew her nose. "While you are away, I want to start a network blog on what we have discovered to share with my scientific colleagues. I want to find out what they already know and how much of this correlates with what is actually happening."

"Great idea," said Sam. "I'll talk to some of my contacts about doing a program on it as well. We could really raise awareness of what's going on. Most people have absolutely no idea."

"Do you think it matters if they do or not?" asked Penny.

"I think that it helps to be aware of changes that may be coming up, and try to understand the positive aspects of them," he replied. "Also, if it's important to steer away from negative emotions to get through the process, it may help if people know it's just part of their evolutionary progress. The last thing we need it to have any kind of blockage due to fear."

"That's very true," Penny replied. "Our society is programmed to dismiss these kinds of ideas as 'crackpot' theories. This is the time to start thinking outside the square. Before it's too late."

Chapter 34

Charles, Linda's tall and solidly built husband, was at Cape Town airport waiting for them as they walked through customs. "Daddy!" shouted Joshua and Indigo as they ran towards him. He bent over and scooped them up in his arms, smiling broadly.

After packing their luggage in the car, they left the airport and headed to Camp's Bay where Charles and Linda lived. They didn't take any notice of the limousine following them at a discreet distance.

Charles dropped them off and then drove about 10 minutes further down the coastal road to Llandudno, where Trish lived.

"How was it?" he asked as the car pulled up outside her house.

"A wonderful break, thank you. Linda and the kids had a fantastic time, as did I," replied Trish.

She wasn't about to go into the details with Charles about what happened. It was bad enough trying to tell Linda, who had a tendency to dismiss anything that she could not explain. Charles was the archetypal conservative man.

Charles dropped her bags into the house and quickly sped off again, to Trish's relief. She needed some time to herself after 10 days with Linda and the kids.

She poured herself a glass of water and went to sit out on the terrace. The sun was just setting on the ocean, in one of the most glorious sunsets she had ever seen. She shut her eyes and started to meditate.

That night, she had a dream about Indigo. Her little granddaughter was talking to her telepathically. They were conversing easily through their minds without any need to speak. Indigo was telling her not to worry about her, and that she was here on Earth to help with the transition.

I always knew there was more to Indigo than we thought, said Trish to herself when she woke up.

While she was still lying in bed, the phone rang shrilly.

It was Linda asking if she wanted to come over to dinner that evening. Trish sighed. Linda was probably worried that she might be feeling lonely, which was far from the truth. In reality, Trish had always enjoyed her own company. Adrian used to travel so much anyway, she had got used to it over the years.

After a swim in the pool, Trish dried herself off and went into the kitchen to prepare some breakfast. She switched on the TV and the 24-hour news channel came on. She looked at the news in dismay. After 10 days without a TV, it was a shock to see what was going on in the world. There was a new set of natural disasters, flooding and more earthquakes.

More signs, Trish thought to herself. *I don't think this is going to get any better.* She switched the TV off and decided to have a media fast for a while. It wasn't that she wanted to block out the world, it was just that the news was never presented in the right way. It always made her feel powerless and sad, rather than inspired to take positive action.

We need media that will empower and inform us, not drain our energy and our hope, she thought.

Trish decided to take a walk on the beach. As she walked along the sand, she pondered on the meaning of man's connection with fellow humans, and the Earth. Looking at the waves crashing onto the shore, she sensed the presence of Mother Earth, eternal Nature, and her power.

What are we doing to you?, she asked. *Our endless desire for wealth and material possessions has caused untold damage to the planet. We don't realize that we are doing this to ourselves. The Earth will survive just fine without us, but we may not for much longer if we continue to plunder at this rate.*

Chapter 35

Later that afternoon, Trish drove over to Linda and Charles's house in Camp's Bay. They had a stunning house overlooking the beach, and had witnessed many glorious sunsets over the decade they had owned it.

Linda had set up the table outside on the terrace for dinner, and Charles was lighting the Braai. There were freshly caught king prawns, juicy steaks, and spicy Sosatie kebabs ready to cook. Indigo and Joshua were on the beach running around and playing.

"G&T, Mom?" asked Linda, although she already knew the answer. She brought the drinks out of the kitchen and laid them on the table facing the beach. "It's beautiful, isn't it?" said Linda, as she watched her mother admiring the sunset. "Still, it was nice to see the sun rise every morning in Mexico, for a change," she added. "It was a great holiday, Mom, thanks again."

Trish smiled warmly at her daughter. "You are welcome, my dear. It was entirely my pleasure. And what a wonderful experience at Chichen Itza."

Linda furrowed her brow. "You don't really believe all that stuff, do you, Mom?" she asked. "It really is some of the most farfetched mumbo jumbo I have ever heard. And I thought Cape Town was bad enough," she added, referring to all the New Age groups in the area.

"Look, I agree with you on one level," replied Trish. "There is too much New Age hype around at the moment, and some of it's just plain commercial. But that doesn't mean that everything about this movement is rubbish. There's a risk that the important truths are being diluted, distorted, and trivialized. I wish we could have a serious conversation about this one day, when Charles is not around."

Charles had a tendency to be particularly scornful of anything alternative or that he didn't understand, and he had a huge influence over Linda.

"You can hardly blame him, Mom," replied Linda. "Remember when you told him that Indigo had incarnated on Earth from another planet? No wonder he thinks you are a kook."

"Dinner's ready, folks," called out Charles cheerfully from behind the Braai. He was busy piling the char-grilled steak, prawns, and kebabs onto a large serving platter.

They all sat down at the dinner table and started to help themselves. Trish asked Charles how his company expansion was going. He had just launched new branches of his security business in Johannesburg and Durban. Linda had almost left him because he had barely been home for a year.

"Well, thank you," he replied. *I'm glad it's all in place at last.* "I hope to increase profits by 300% by the end of this year. That should pay for Linda's expensive taste in clothes and my new BMW," he laughed.

Trish smiled and looked down at her prawns. *Things they really need*, she thought to herself. *Are they really worth it?*

Leaving their house that evening, Trish wondered about how Charles and Linda would survive if all that the Elders foretold was going to happen.

Chapter 36

That night, Trish had a vivid dream. She was sitting in a temple when a light-filled being approached her and sat down. He began to speak:

"I have the third message for you and your tribe.

"As we lead up to the Great Transition, more and more mediums, religious groups, spiritual societies and esoteric organizations are claiming to be inspired by contact with great masters, light beings, angels and archangels.

"Trust your intuition and listen to what they say with discernment. Although many are genuine, some of these people are accessing the astral plane, which is the home to both positive and negative entities, and they may unknowingly channel an entity that may be altering the truth.

"Others have become consumed with their own self-importance, as their egos have elevated them – in their own minds – above others in ability and knowledge.

"Listen to yourselves. You will know the true messengers by their kind and non-egoistic disposition, and by their messages filled with love, compassion and wisdom. The time of blind following of others is past, this is the time to recognize that the answers lie within."

When Trish woke up the next morning, she passed the message onto the group. It wasn't long before she received a chat message from Aurelie.

Hi Trish. That's very interesting, and not something I would have thought about before. I have always assumed that anybody involved in spirituality must automatically be one of the 'good guys', and I had never thought that they might be influenced by misleading entities. Food for thought.

Trish. We have to be careful. I must have received this message because I have been to a lot of these workshops and meetings and I am starting to see major ego issues with some of the facilitators. Particularly when they claim that the path to 'ascension' can be achieved by paying them a lot of money!

Aurelie. Yes I know what you mean, it is coming back to the whole concept of 'handing over your power' that the Elders warned us about. There's no doubt that some of these people can be helpful, but we need to start developing our own powers of intuition and seeing ourselves as powerful beings as well, all capable of accessing information.

Trish. Agree. Now that we have received three messages, there seems to be a pattern developing that runs along the theme of us waking up to our own power, and taking responsibility for our own lives.

Aurelie. And the role of music as well. I can't wait to hear the next messages – like pieces of a jigsaw puzzle being slowly put together. No doubt with an enlightening conclusion.

Trish. Yes, one that will no doubt shake the foundations of our belief systems. I just hope that we can make the changes we need to make before the Earth upheavals start in earnest. I have to go, but let's chat again soon.

Chapter 37

It was the full moon on Friday night, so Trish set off for her monthly group meditation near Table Mountain. After she parked her car, Trish entered the hall and sat down on one of the chairs in the front row. She admired the beautiful display of crystals laid out on a purple throw in the centre of the room, surrounded by several candles. As usual, there was a wonderful smell of incense in the room.

"Welcome to our monthly meditation," said Meredith, the pleasant woman who ran the meditation group. Trish liked Meredith, because she seemed more genuine than did some of the others in the New Age movement in Cape Town.

Meredith continued. "Let us begin our meditation for world peace."

The group shut their eyes and focused on their breath.

"Imagine a beautiful column of white light above your heads," said Meredith. "Bring this column of light through your crown and into your bodies, and be filled with vibrant white light. As this light fills you, channel it out of your right hand into a large column of light in the middle of the room. You are harnessing the unlimited loving energy of the Universe.

"Now imagine this huge column of loving energy moving to all the areas of dark on the Earth, and filling them with light and healing. Send it to all of the zones of war, to all your friends, and all your enemies. Let it cover the entire Earth with its soft, loving mist. Visualize the world as healed."

Suddenly, a woman in the group stood up and started to speak in a strange, guttural voice:

"Dear ones,

"It is no coincidence that you are all here today. You are Warriors of the Light, who have come to clear the weeds of ignorance and help usher in a new world age. Although by nature you are loving and kind, you will also fight without reservation to free humanity from its vibratory imprisonment and veil of delusion.

"Your actions, indeed your very presence as your energies rise in this age is bringing dishonesty, corruption, and greed to the surface so that it may be dissolved in the light. You are being given the opportunity to penetrate the veil of forgetfulness by meeting each other and invoking the group-soul that connects you.

"Now is the time to seek out others like you and work together to achieve this magnificent objective.

"You will recognize each other through the following characteristics:

"Firstly, you may have a sense of important duty to perform, to help humanity. You may feel different in some way from others, not part of the crowd.

"Some, especially the younger among you, may have afflictions due to the Earth's lower psychic climate, such as attention deficit disorder, obsessive compulsive disorder, autism, and allergies, and this can lead to overuse of sedatives such as alcohol, drugs, or food.

"You may have an acute sensitivity to the thoughts and feelings of others, as well as psychic phenomena.

"Some of you have been affected by traumatic events while still young and impressionable, perpetrated by the darker forces who have tried to make it harder for you to fulfill your purpose.

"You have the ability to transmute energies due to empathy, overcoming fear or selfishness with love channeled through you from higher planes. You are more focused on humanity's spiritual growth rather than that of any individual.

"You are by nature frank and direct, which may lead to unwarranted hostility from others. Although this skill is useful in exposing the truth, it can also teach you that silent compassion and loving thoughts can provide better service at times.

"Many of you have reflective auras that mirror and expose the issues of others, leading to irrational antagonism from them. This is something that some of you have perhaps never understood.

"The women among you tend to attract weaker men, who may drain you of energy and take actions that may try to weaken or disempower you.

"You display a rapid and sympathetic response to suffering, and have a sense of justice, dedication to truth, righteousness, contemplative intelligence, passion to learn, and intuition.

"Finally, you have a clear recognition of need for unity and the union of many to achieve a single and selfless goal, rather than a following of any individual guru.

"Gather together where you can, as your efforts will be amplified when you work together. "

The woman opened her eyes suddenly and stopped speaking.

Trish and the rest of the group slowly opened their eyes. She felt incredibly peaceful. She looked at Meredith and asked if she could speak. Meredith nodded warmly.

"I had an experience in Mexico recently, where I met a group of people who seem to have many of the characteristics of the Warriors of Light. We were told by a group of Elders that we had decided to help humanity to make the transition from one era to the next, and that the turning point would be in 2012."

Meredith smiled. "I do believe that we are nearing the end of a great cycle, and that those who have learned the necessary lessons will be elevated into a higher level of experience."

"Do you mean the kind of 'ascension' that some yogis have achieved?" asked a woman at the back.

"Yes, except that this time everybody will have the opportunity to ascend in consciousness, because the new Aquarian Energies will make it much easier," replied Meredith. "The key to success will be through our vibration, which will need to be raised to a minimal level to allow us to graduate to the next. Jesus called this the 'Sifting Time,' the Koran 'Kiyamat,' leading to what Mayan Prophecy calls the 'Golden Age.'"

"What about people whose vibrations are not sufficiently raised?" asked Marie.

"I believe that the new world consciousness will be unsuitable for them," said Meredith. "This is because the more intense energy will just amplify their negative tendencies and hold back the progress of more advanced souls. They may move to other worlds where they will continue to learn life's lessons. It will be their choice. We all have that choice."

Chapter 38

Trish's mind was spinning as she drove home to Llandudno later that evening. It was a very clear night, brightly illuminated by the full moon. She parked her car in the drive, and decided to make herself a cup of chamomile tea before retiring.

She took her tea out to the terrace, wrapping herself in her turquoise shawl for warmth. As she gazed out to the ocean, she thought about the woman who channeled information that night, and understood for the first time why she and the others had been chosen by the Elders.

They were among the many 'Warriors of Light' who were coming together to help usher in the New World. She wondered what the future held, and what kinds of physical changes would take place. Should she move to higher ground?

Her mind then flashed back to something the Elders had said in Cancun: "The greatest changes during the birth of the New World shall be in the inner planes, not from the external or physical plane, which will just be outward symptoms of internal turmoil. So it matters not where you are in the world, and taking shelter of a material form may not protect you from the impending storm."

It's all about what's going on inside, she thought to herself. *It's so important, yet so few people actually understand.* She wished there was some way she could get the message through to others, to get them to see the truth, in its purest form.

Trish decided that night to set up an international network to promote the message she had received from the Elders. She would use her extensive connections with leading spiritual leaders all over the world to support and make their followers aware of the movement. She would involve Indigo as well.

She was already visualizing the new website she would set up, with the help of her hi-tech friend next door. It would be a glorious turquoise, the Mayan sacred blue, which was reputed to attune the physical to the higher realms, balancing the mind and soul, and connecting with all life.

Trish closed her eyes and smiled, blissfully unaware that she was being observed by a man looking through a telescope from an adjoining house. He had been monitoring her emails and had just seen the chat messages between her and Aurelie.

As he sent off his report, he smiled coldly. *Harmless for now, but it will escalate,* he thought. *She is one of Them, and doesn't realize her power yet. Let's hope she never does...*

Chapter 39

"Are you crazy?" Tom Barton, Jr., strode furiously into the meeting room at J.P. Morland where Guy was waiting to see him. "What the hell are you thinking including employee feedback that we might have set them up? I didn't ask you to play Sherlock Holmes, just work on the merger of the two organizations."

"Just doing my job," replied Guy. "It's part of the due diligence. I can't just leave it out—you know it doesn't work that way."

"I don't care how you do it, just do it," said Tom. "If you don't change the report, then I'm afraid that that you will have to face the consequences."

Guy's report had identified that Beal Stantons was in better shape than J.P. Morland in terms of sub-prime exposure before the takeover. Even worse, that J.P. Morland had been on the brink of collapse because of its high derivatives exposure. The $60 billion injection of taxpayer money via the Fed enabled it to save itself while acquiring its arch rival.

At the same time, the report suggested that it allowed insiders to take large "short" positions in Beal Stantons' stocks, thereby collecting huge profits. Guy's employer, a major business consulting firm, was obliged by financial laws to report any information discovered through due diligence and employee feedback.

Tom's reaction confirms that it's all true, thought Guy as he walked out of the meeting room. He made his way to the lift that would take him down to the lobby. His mind was spinning, in a complete dilemma. If he took all the employee comments out and other information he had discovered, it would change the report entirely, including the findings and conclusions.

As he let himself into his apartment, he decided to drive to New Jersey for the weekend. He would see if David was available to join him. It had been a while since they had been to their comfortable cottage on the beach.

Guy parked the car next to the Cape Cod style beach cottage and David jumped out quickly. "I'll get the bags if you want to go out and get some food," he said.

That suited Guy, who loved choosing what they would eat for dinner. He had a particular liking for the fresh seafood that was available at the local fish shop. He was mentally choosing the menus for the weekend as he drove away.

When he returned to the cottage, David had packed away their clothes and was sitting on the deck overlooking the beach with a glass of wine in his hands. "Hope you got something tasty for dinner," he said with a twinkle in his eye. "I'm starving."

Guy had bought some extra provisions because he was going to stay on for a few days to rework the project. His employer, Sanderson Consulting, did not want to risk falling out with J.P. Morland, one of the most powerful investment banks in the world. He had been categorically told to make the adjustments that J.P. Morland had asked for.

David lit the barbecue to cook the fresh fish that Guy had bought at the local shop as they watched the sky turn a yellowy pink. David glanced over at Guy. "You look tired," he said. "Are you still mad about what happened?"

"The whole thing stinks," said Guy. "I'm finding it really hard to compromise my professional integrity like this. But," he said with a rueful smile, "they have left me with no other choice. Change the report or I'm fired."

David scooped up the pieces of fish and placed them on their plates. He took a sip of his glass of wine. "Hey, think about this for a couple of days before you decide. Don't make any hasty decisions either way. Remember, jobs come and go, but you have to live with yourself forever. Decide what is more important. You know I'll support whatever decision you make."

Guy smiled. David had an inner wisdom that never ceased to amaze him.

Chapter 40

That night, Guy had a strange dream, in which a man that resembled the Elder from Mexico spoke to him.

"I have the 4th message for your tribe.

"Your present society is run by a small group of powerful people, who are trying to prevent you from reaching your full potential, so that they can maintain ultimate power. They cannot continue to dominate and control you if you see through the illusion of the world, and realize that you are fully capable of changing it through your collective thoughts.

"To prevent you from waking up at this critical time, they have orchestrated the world economic collapse to generate misery and depression worldwide. This is designed to keep your vibrations low. And because they are losing power, governments are trying to control and monitor humanity under the guise of protection from terrorists.

"As we lead up to the Great Transition everything is becoming more extreme. Love, beauty, humanity, and compassion are being heightened, but so are fear, brutality, pain, disease, anxiety, greed, corruption, and materialism.

"This corrupt and unsustainable system must be exposed and brought into the light to be healed. They cannot win against an empowered and aware humanity. Remember, everything in the universe is part of the greater whole. It is the dark side of humanity, which exists in us all, that needs to be drawn out and healed.

"Some of you will be given the opportunity to expose and topple them. For too long, any criticism has been quashed either by assassination, or by discrediting the sources. But the darker energies supporting their greed and exploitation are being transmuted and withdrawn, as we move into the Aquarian Age.

"But be careful: by exposing the truth, you will be in great danger. You will be observed and monitored, and if you start to endanger their plans they will be ruthless. So be wary, but know that we are also here to guide and assist you, you only need to ask."

Guy woke up suddenly, in a sweat. He shook David to wake him up, then wrote down as much as he could remember on an email and sent it to the group.

Chapter 41

The next morning, while David was out jogging on the beach, Guy checked his emails and saw a response from Yasmin about his dream.

Hi Guy,

That dream confirms what we already thought, doesn't it? There is a lot at stake here. The warning is clearly there as well. After I got your email, I asked a guy I know from my old department to check my apartment and computer. He specializes in bugging and debugging. You will never guess what he found? There were hidden cameras, listening devices, you name it! My computer had an 'undetectable' monitoring program that was recording all my activity and transferring it remotely to an email address. It seems incredible – I mean, we haven't actually done anything yet! Why are we being targeted? Do they know something we don't? I guess if the projects we are planning come to fruition, they could endanger their plans.

I think we need to warn the others to be vigilant and also get their computers and apartments checked. Aurelie may need to move to a secret location, as she is isolated in the countryside. I'll send them emails and let them know what I found, and what they can do to protect themselves.

I'll keep you posted.

Yasmin

Guy shook his head in astonishment. It was like being in a movie, except it was real. He rang an left a message for a friend who specialized in surveillance, asking him to check his apartment in New York, as well as the Cape Cod house, and their computers and phones.

While he was waiting to hear back from him, Guy did a search on the Internet on the latest news on the bank. An article written by a highly respected stock option specialist came up entitled "Beal Stantons Buyout Complete Fraud." Curious, he scrolled down the page to read the article:

All the evidence points to the fact that the demise of Beal Stantons was orchestrated to allow the payment of $60 billion of taxpayer money to J.P. Morland, and enable insiders to take large 'short' positions in Beal stock and gain enormous profits. The idea that rumours caused a 'run on the bank' at Beal is unfounded, and being used as an excuse to cover up one of the most outrageous frauds of the decade.

Another confirmation, thought Guy. *Why isn't the FED investigating?*

Guy clicked onto his Yahoo account to check his private mail. A news headline on his home page captured his attention: "John Garner Resigns over Prostitution Scandal." He had always admired John Garner, former attorney general, for his pursuit of corporate corruption and defence of the common man. The article described how Garner had been caught arranging a "tawdry" hotel liaison with high-class call girl. Guy smiled. *Hypocrites*, he thought. Half of New York's business and political elite has probably done the same thing—they just didn't get caught. His many enemies on Wall Street must be delighted.

Guy suddenly remembered who else might be pleased to see him go. Garner had written a scathing article about unregulated predatory lending practices that were crippling home buyers. He claimed that the government had chosen to align itself with the banks by rendering all state predatory lending laws inoperative and preventing any new consumer protection laws from being passed. *Why didn't any of the press report on that?* He thought. *He wrote that article only a couple of months before this happened. It sounds like an uncanny coincidence.*

David suddenly appeared at the door, sweaty and smiling after his morning run. "Come on, take a break," he said sternly. Guy smiled and switched off his computer. They spent the rest of the day unwinding and basking in the sun.

Later that evening, after David had left for New York, Guy sat on the couch with a glass of wine and thought about what he had discovered that morning. *I'm seeing things I never saw before*, he realized. *It's as if I am waking up to possibilities I would have completely dismissed in the past.*

Guy had always prided himself on his ability to analyze the facts and draw sensible and rational conclusions. Those qualities had made him an excellent business consultant. But for the first time in his life, he was starting to question his beliefs.

Chapter 42

The next morning, Guy decided to do some more research. He emailed his friend John, a former J.P. Morland banker who had made his fortune several years before and was living a life of luxury in Bermuda. John had always talked about the elite group controlling business, banking, and government. Guy had dismissed John's views, although he had a huge amount of respect for his intelligence and business acumen.

Dear John,

How are you? Hey, I need your advice about something. Since working on the J.P. Morland assignment, I've noticed some strange goings-on that seem to indicate an agenda by the elite banking families. I remember you used to talk about this group and a New World Order they were planning. Can you fill me in again?

Thanks,

Guy

After about 15 minutes, John's reply appeared in his mailbox.

Hey Guy,

Great to hear from you!

Well, I was wondering how long it would take you to wake up to this!

There is a great deal of evidence, some of which I have seen firsthand, to indicate that a small group of people have been covertly controlling many aspects of our lives for some time. This group, sometimes referred to as the Global Elite, or the Illuminati, is as you mentioned composed of powerful banking dynasties and other powerful entities.

Some say that they are behind a long-term plan to introduce a world government, the "New World Order." They are already controlling us through the massive debts that we incur to live a lifestyle they encourage us to aspire to. They control the media via the huge global corporations they own, feeding us with what they want us to see and hear. They control all the candidates we elect to government through political donations, and if they stand up to them, they get rid them. John F. Kennedy wanted to abolish the Federal Reserve, which would have reduced their control over money. More recently, Garner, who wrote that scathing article about how the government colluded with the banks to abolish the laws to protect consumers from sub-prime lending, was forced to resign because they exposed him for seeing a prostitute.

They control the movie and music studios so that they can feed the young with what they want them to see and hear.

This world government plan started centuries ago, and is only now almost reaching fruition. The United Nations was their first attempt, but it hasn't been very successful. The Trilateral Commission founded in 1973 gave rise to economic globalization.

They are now creating regional government groups such as the European Union and the North American Union, which have greater control than the UN. Have you heard of the North American Union, an "EU" style community between Canada, the U.S., and Mexico? It was set up recently without congressional approval.

Creating a global currency is also part of the plan. It was the Euro first, and now a new currency for the North American Union called the Amero is planned. If they are successful, a single global currency will come next, as the regional currencies strengthen at the expense of individual currencies. Many of these decisions are made at the annual meeting of the Bilderberg Group, which has been called the most exclusive and secretive club in the world. You are only admitted if you run a multinational bank, giant corporation, or a country!

What's most fascinating is that they get us to agree to everything they introduce by creating situations that cause us to act predictably.

For example, they justified the war in Iraq by telling us that Saddam was sheltering terrorists and weapons of mass destruction. As we all now know, none of it was real. It was really about securing Iraq's oil supplies. Iran may well be next, under the guise of a supposed nuclear threat. The war on terror was created to continue removing peoples' civic liberties, under the guise of protecting them against terrorists. They are manipulating the "terrorists" as much as the rest of us.

The current sub-prime debacle is another example, where they deliberately loaned money to people who couldn't afford it, and are now foreclosing on their houses and creating untold misery. By the way, they have done the same thing several times over the past century; they call it the "boom and bust" cycle.

The situation will become so untenable that the next step will be to introduce much tighter financial regulation, which supports the concept of a single currency and global bank. People will welcome more regulation to avoid having to go through that again.

One of the scariest parts of the plan is to introduce an RFID chip under the skin of everybody in the world, with all their money and information on it. As it is, all new U.S. passports are implanted with these chips. As someone was recently quoted saying, 'If people want to protest about what we do or violate what we want, we just turn off the chip.'"

Guy, I hope this helps. If we don't all wake up to this, I hate to think what kind of world our children will inherit, and within a very short period of time.

Best,

John

Guy sat back in his chair, his mind racing from what he had just read. *Surely this can't be true*, he thought to himself. He started thinking about all of the points John made, comparing them with what he already knew about the credit crunch, new computer implant technology, security measures, tightening controls, government ID cards.

Yes it can, he concluded. *It already is.*

Chapter 43

The next morning, Guy put a call through to his office, telling them that he would not compromise his professional integrity by changing the report. They would need to get somebody else to do it. He realized that he would no longer be able to work at Sanderson as a result.

He sat at his desk, thinking through what to do next. He decided to reply to John's email.

Dear John,

Thanks for your email. I'm starting to realize that this is not just some fantasist theory, but that it's probably real. Just today, the papers are reporting that the Senate has approved a new bill to broaden wiretap powers and providing legal immunity for the phone companies that cooperate with the National Security Agency. As it is, I also found out our own places had been wired and our computers hijacked. We have now debugged and installed powerful new anti-spy software.

Let's do something about it. Let's raise awareness among our friends and colleagues. I'm prepared to go public with the information I have, even if I risk prosecution. It's risky, but someone has to do it. We've been in the dark for too long.

Guy

Later that evening, David walked into the cottage and came over to give Guy a hug. "Tough decision, but the right one," he said. "We'll get through this together."

Guy replied thoughtfully. "I want to take this further," he said. "I want to start an awareness campaign aimed at people like you and I. In the past, this kind of information has been restricted to underground websites that attract the interest of typical 'conspiracy theorists'. I need to make this credible. I'm setting something up with John Saber, who used to work for J.P. Morland but now lives in Bermuda. He is highly respected by the business community."

"There's one thing I really don't understand," said David. "Can you explain how this group are controlling the current economy? Why on earth would a financial crisis be in their best interests?"

Guy walked over to the fridge, and pulled out a bottle of wine. He poured two glasses and took them out to the terrace overlooking the beach.

"In a nutshell, currencies are not created by the central banks to cover the interest owed on debts," he replied. "So there is never enough money in circulation to pay off the original debt plus the accruing interest of that debt. So the 'fiat' system as they call it requires a debt 'bubble' that can never be paid off, and this allows them to keep milking the debt bubble to their advantage, expanding it and floating through means such as derivatives. None of this is based on real market fundamentals.

"The only solution to deal with this huge amount of individual, corporate, and government debt is via a controlled and orchestrated economic collapse," Guy continued. "The bankers then take all the real assets, such as real estate, natural resources, etc., for a fraction of their original price. They count on people's desperation to survive. Then they start all over again."

Chapter 44

It's great to be home, thought Laurel to herself as the plane taxied on the runway at Sydney airport. Those warm feelings she always had whenever she came home resurfaced. Her elder sister Joanne would be at the airport waiting for her, and would drive her back to her apartment in Mosman.

The lady at passport control cracked a joke as she presented her passport. *Why are Aussies so laid back compared to Europeans?* she asked herself. *Must be the climate; guess it's so warm there's no point in worrying.*

Joanne was waiting for her as she walked out with her luggage. She gave her sister a hug. "It's been too long, Sis."

"Yes, I know," Laurel replied. She was glad to be home. It was a great adventure, but now it was time to think about it all. She was pleased that Sam had stayed a few extra days in London with Penny.

As they drove back to her apartment, Laurel filled her sister in on some of the highlights of her trip. She was exhausted, and when they arrived she decided to go straight to bed to catch up on some sleep.

The next day, Laurel drove out to her weekender in the country, just 1½ hours from Sydney. She had bought a little cottage on a 5-acre plot a few years before, set just outside the tiny historic town of Wollombi in the Hunter Valley. It was the only place she felt really at home.

She drove her car up the steep entry ramp and parked it at the side of the house. It was exactly as she had left it, six months before. Her boyfriend Campbell, who owned the property next door, had kept it in perfect condition for her return.

She had missed him as well. He was pretty special, and a good match for her. They shared a love for the bush, and were both passionate about sustainable lifestyles. She was looking forward to seeing him that night, as he was flying back from a business trip that afternoon, and taking a few days off work to spend time with her in the country.

Laurel carried her bags into the house, then took a beer out of the fridge and sat back on her couch. *Might put the fire on tonight*, she thought. It was strange jumping from one season to another within a couple of days, although the English summer that year wasn't too dissimilar to the Australian winter.

Her eyes glanced over at the bookcase that lined an entire wall of her lounge room. There were a lot of books there that she had never read, that her sister had left with her when she left to live in Perth. Her eyes stopped at a book called The Phenomenon of Man, written by the French paleontologist and Jesuit priest Pierre

Teilhard de Chardin. She remembered her sister had told her that he had believed in the existence of a "thinking membrane" enveloping the Earth. A bit like Jung's collective unconscious.

She pulled it off the shelf and opened the book at the section headed "The Law of Complexity/Consciousness." *Interesting*, she thought. *He is saying that there is a tendency for matter to become more complex and at the same time increase in consciousness, as observed by evolution.* She skipped through the pages, and her eyes stopped at a paragraph:

Through population growth, and greater social contact with others within the closed and circular surface of the Earth, we are evolving towards an Omega Point of consciousness, or the Noosphere. At this point, consciousness will rupture through time and space and assert itself on a higher plane of existence from which it cannot return.

That's sounds similar to some of the messages coming through, thought Laurel.

She decided to do some up-to-date research on the Internet on the Noosphere. That word had cropped up a few times lately. A site commenting on Teilhard's theories came up, and she started reading:

If as Teilhard suggested there is a thinking membrane surrounding the Earth, and that membrane needs a mechanical infrastructure to support the evolutionary shift towards complexity, then he may have predicted the advent of the Internet.

Once we ascend to the ultimate point in consciousness that de Chardin described, the Noosphere may awaken, and humanity will be aware of its interconnectedness with itself and Nature. We won't need the Internet any more, because this new evolutionary stage will replace it by providing automatic information exchanges including telepathic communication, perhaps in a vastly advanced version of the social networking sites on the Internet operate today.

Fascinating, she thought. *Sounds like the field of collective human consciousness is achieving its final stage of the awakening process.*

Laurel fell asleep soon afterwards, exhausted by the trip.

Chapter 45

Laurel woke up from her nap feeling refreshed, and looked at the clock. It was 5.30pm. She had slept practically all day.

Campbell was driving to Wollombi that evening and they had agreed to meet at the local pub at 6.30 before he came home.

Laurel slipped on a pair of tight jeans and a warm sweater, and looked at herself admiringly in the mirror. *I look pretty good*, she thought. She looked far more relaxed than when she had left for South America 6 months ago.

Campbell was waiting in the pub for her when she arrived. She ran up to him and he picked her up and swung her around in a bear hug. "I've missed you," he said gently. "Me too," Laurel replied. They had only spoken a few times by phone since her departure, and still had a lot of catching up to do.

They ordered some food and sat in the comfortable sofa near the fire. Campbell poured them a glass of red wine. "Tell me all the details of your trip," he said with a twinkle in his eye. "Am I getting a Tango lesson later this evening?"

Laurel laughed, then took a long breath. *Where do I start*, she thought.

She filled him in on her experiences in South America. She decided not to tell him exactly what happened in Mexico until she had another glass of wine, in case she lost her nerve.

Their food arrived, but Laurel just picked at it. Her travels had reduced her appetite considerably, because the local foods had affected her digestion badly.

Campbell poured them another glass of wine, and sat back in the sofa. "Eat a bit more dinner," he said. "You have lost so much weight."

"I just can't keep it down," replied Laurel. "Anyway, I'll have plenty of time to fatten up after a few of your delicious home-cooked meals," she said with a smile.

"Campbell, do you remember what I told you on the phone about that experience in Mexico," she asked. "You don't still think I've gone completely around the bend, do you?"

Campbell laughed heartily. "No I was just teasing you. You are starting to sound like your sister – she always had some unusual ideas! I'd be interested in knowing more about what happened."

Laurel nodded her head. "Remember the panic I was in before the millennium, which ended being a big anticlimax?"

Campbell remembered it well. Laurel had been convinced that the world was on the verge of an environmental disaster. She had insisted that they spend the millennium holed up at his remote cabin in the woods, equipped with several months' supply of water and canned foods. He still had a few dozen cans of sardines from 1999 well past their use-by date.

"Yes I do," he replied dryly. "Are you saying there's another one in the cards?" he asked with a twinkle in his eyes. "I still have some provisions from the last one."

"Not exactly, but something like that," replied Laurel cautiously. "The Elders talked about a new era we are entering in or around 2012, which is the culmination of an evolutionary stage in our development.

It is apparently linked with the growth of a geometrical electromagnetic field surrounding the Earth that has also been called the "Unity Consciousness Grid." It is a kind of a door into a higher dimension, which we are apparently all unaware exists at the present time."

"That sounds a bit like the Aboriginal Dreamtime or Dreaming," said Campbell. "They refer to it as a space we all go in and out of in more or less conscious ways in our lives. Johnny's here. Let's get him over to talk about it a bit more."

Campbell waved at an elderly Aboriginal man standing by the bar, inviting him to come over and sit with them.

"How are you, mate?" he asked with a broad smile. Johnny would help him out on his farm quite often, when he wasn't going 'walkabout'.

"As well as can be," replied Johnny. "How are you folks this evening?"

"We need to pick your brains about Dreamtime, Johnny," said Campbell. "What can you tell us?"

"Mate, Dreamtime is the dream space, the Dreaming of our lives," said Johnny. "It is the shared dream between all our peoples. It is a creative space we call the 'all-at-once time', where we experience past, present and future at the same time. It is everywhere but nowhere. We relax into it and allow the stories to unfold."

He looked out of the window, gazing towards the sky. "Our fathers spoke of the original story, the story of harmony that involves every person, not just the aboriginal. In this story, we all made a choice at a time of creation to be in harmony and to participate in the shared dream.

"The dream space is created by our stories, our dreams, memories, knowings, symbols, and tools," Johnny continued.

"It is a creative space, where possibilities unfold and recreate within the consciousness of your own mind. If you use the dream space in a creative way, then you can shape your destiny in a conscious way."

"How can you use it creatively?" asked Laurel.

"By meditating, quieting your mind of thoughts that distract you. Find that quiet space and you will discover a real knowledge that will affect your entire life. This is the power of our shared dream."

Laurel and Campbell drove back to her cottage later that evening. "I'd like to start meditating to tap into the Dreaming," said Laurel. "I've spent my whole life avoiding looking inside," she continued, "because I was always so busy and distracted getting on with life. My mind has done a great job in keeping me occupied with so many external things."

Campbell nodded. "Sometimes we don't want to slow down in case our inner voice tells us something we don't want to hear," he said. "Before I bought my place up here, I had forgotten my secret, inner dreams. Now I realize that the part of me that comes out when I am here, is my authentic self. That's why I am so happy when I am here. Took me years to figure it out."

They lit the fire and had a nightcap before going to bed. Campbell started stroking Laurel's hair as she snuggled up to him on the couch. "I'm never leaving you again," she whispered, as he tightened his arms around her.

Chapter 46

That night, Laurel had a vivid dream in which a light being spoke to her.

"I have the fifth message for you and your tribe.

"After the Great Transition, as Awakened Beings, you will function naturally, instinctively, and perfectly. Much like sophisticated computers, you will be equipped with data analysis systems assessing all the factors present at any given time.

"These will enable you to choose the best course of action every time, one that offers the least resistance and the greatest fulfillment. Evolving beyond the notion of human-made linear time, you will be able to slow down or speed up the passage of time. This will bring the return of universal telepathy, heightened senses, and full consciousness.

"The field of collective human consciousness that surrounds the Earth will have achieved its final stage of the awakening process, and become a single planetary being connecting everything.

"The rational thought processes that have frequently led you along the wrong path will no longer override your inner wisdom. You will instinctively discover your true purpose by attuning to inner feelings, vibrations, and planetary rhythms. You will fulfill these roles as individual, musical notes in an exquisitely balanced symphony.

"Your roles in the transition will be to keep this vision before the eyes of humanity; educate mankind regarding the most urgent issues of the day; to guide others towards a realization of their own innate divinity; to inspire mankind to fulfill its destined work of planetary service; to restore balance and help heal planet Earth; to receive illumination from the higher worlds and share this to further mankind's spiritual interests; to act as a bridge between old and new, by receiving light and power from above and use it to eradicate evil, reinstate virtue, anchor the new Aquarian frequencies into the physical plane, and so help build the new world.

"But heed these words. Whether they wish it or not, whether they understand it or not, every person today will be compelled to make a choice. The choice will be determined not by what they say, but what they do, and this will be evident in the vibratory rate of consciousness they manifest.

"This will indicate whether they have opted to move forward with the new and vital, or have chosen to stay with the old and redundant ways of being.

"The Spirit Force is a vibrant, playful energy that wants you to dance, sing, and enjoy its glorious creation. This is a wonderful time to be alive!

Chapter 47

Laurel woke up the next morning and remembered the dream. Before sending it out to the group, she dwelled on some of what the being had said. *We have a key role to play here,* she thought. *And it sounds like we are all in this together.*

Laurel got up quietly, careful not to disturb Campbell, and switched on her computer to send the message out to the group. She picked up the email about the surveillance and decided to wait until she had her computer checked.

She went outside while she waited for Campbell to wake up, so that she could alert him to the possibility that there could be a listening device in the cottage.

She opened the French doors and walked out onto her terrace. She sat down on her wicker chair and looked out at the green valley below. *It's so peaceful here*, she thought. *I'm going to try to meditate.*

Laurel closed her eyes. She focused on her breath, and breathed in to the count of 3, and out to the count of 6. Thoughts came flickering through her head. Really important things like what they were going to have for breakfast.

Slowly, but surely, she let them go by as she continued to focus on her breathing. Finally, she seemed to get to a place where her mind could relax, without being bombarded by thoughts. She decided that her thoughts could wait, for a change.

She sensed a connection with a part of herself that she rarely saw. It was inside her, an inner, knowing part of her. All of a sudden, she imagined a white light coming down through her crown into her body. It was as if it was scanning her, not unlike an antivirus software, and removing anything that shouldn't be there. Then she felt as if she was downloading information, a bit like the automatic updates on the computer. *This is weird*, she thought, *a bit like what they said in the dream.*

After about half an hour, she opened her eyes again. She felt much lighter and calmer than before. *I could get used to this*, she thought. *I think I need a daily connection with the source to update my systems, a bit like a computer needs regular updating.*

Campbell appeared in the doorway, and she put her fingers to her lips, before walking out to the nearby bushland, beckoning him to follow her.

"We could be under surveillance," she whispered. Seeing his incredulous expression, she explained what had happened to the others. "OK, I'll check everything out, including our computers," said Campbell, wondering what on earth was going on.

He didn't find anything in the cottage, but Laurel's computer was bugged. He removed the spyware immediately.

"This is really incredible," he said. "I didn't believe all that stuff you told me but it looks like somebody is very interested in you all and wants to know what you are up to." He walked over to the table and picked up Laurel's laptop.

"They must have bugged all your computers when you were all in London."

Laurel nodded. "It's possible. We didn't really suspect anything at that stage."

"We are going to have to be *very* careful from now on," said Campbell. "I'll set up a secure space on the web that you can communicate through. Nobody will know what you are all doing."

A few days later, Laurel had a meeting with her co-producer. She had already written the outline of the program she was planning on sustainable living, but needed to discuss it with him in more detail. The pilot had already been accepted by a major television channel.

She took the lift up to the 22nd floor of the high rise building, looking behind her in case she was being followed.

Strange being back in civilization, after so many months in the wild, she thought. Laurel loved being in nature, and found the city a very unnatural place. She sometimes felt that the earth was crying out to be free, from underneath all the buildings and cement.

Mervin Johnson was a sustainable living entrepreneur who had made millions developing a new line of eco-friendly cleaning materials. The brand had been successfully extended into many different kinds of products, from camping materials to sheets!

He greeted her at the lift with his arms extended. "Welcome back, my intrepid friend," he said giving her a huge bear hug.

They went through the program in detail, and Laurel talked about the sustainable communities she had visited in South America and the UK. "I have so many new ideas to weave into the show," she said excitedly. "Sam has taken some fantastic footage as well. It is going to be a really, really good program."

Mervin confirmed that he had arranged for the show to air before Christmas that year, depending on Laurel's schedule. "We can do it," she replied airily. "Sam gets back next week, so we'll get started straight away."

"Can't wait to see it come together," said Mervin.

Laurel looked at him thoughtfully. "Mervin," she said, "I want to add something a bit unusual to the content. Something that happened to me when I was in Cancun."

"What is it?" asked Mervin curiously.

"It's about 2012, actually," said Laurel. "A kind of a prophecy. With a conspiracy tale thrown in for good measure."

"It's not that kind of program," said Mervin, trying to look stern. "I hope you aren't just wheeling your millennium ideas out again for good measure?"

"No, this is different," replied Laurel. "It's actually really important. So important that if we don't air it, then the world could be in worse trouble than it is now."

"OK, send me something on it," said Mervin with a smile. "If you twist my arm enough I'm sure we can weave it into the story. Anyway, enough about the series—I'm taking you to lunch. Sydney hasn't been the same without you."

Chapter 48

Leyla took a long puff of the shisha pipe. She loved the strawberry flavor of the tobacco and the gurgling of the water whenever she drew on the pipe.

"I love London," she exclaimed. "It is so civilized."

Leyla and Bahram had just had dinner in their favorite Middle Eastern restaurant in Chelsea. After the meal, they went to one of the outdoor tables to smoke shisha and eat baklava.

"What time are you seeing Li-ying tomorrow?" asked Bahram.

"We are meeting at 10am at the hotel, then going for a walk in Hyde Park," replied Leyla. Leyla had known Li-ying for 15 years. They had met when they had both first come to London as young medical graduates to do an internship at the Chelsea & Westminster Hospital. Li-ying had gone on to set up a clinic devoted to women's health in the centre of London, and had become somewhat of a celebrity as well after writing a book on women, sexuality, and health.

After a few more exchanges of the shisha, Leyla and Bahram returned to their hotel on Park Lane. It was their favorite place to stay when they came to London, despite its extravagant room rates. They fell fast asleep. Leyla had a vivid dream, in which a luminous being spoke to her:

"I have the sixth message for your tribe.

"There has been an extreme patriarchal imbalance on the Earth for a very long time. The innate creative and intuitive qualities of the Feminine Spirit have been long feared by distorted male perception, and as a result women have been repressed, dominated, and persecuted throughout history.

"This imbalance is yet another example of the disharmony being experienced in our present times. The balance needs to be restored, so that the universal symphony can play in perfect harmony.

"To achieve this, the majority of Light Ones on Earth at the moment have chosen to incarnate in female bodies, or in male bodies with a more pronounced feminine side.

"During the lead up to the Great Transition, however, many of you will continue to experience the type of suffering endured by women over the ages, as the male energy fights its last battle to retain its power. However, it will not be long before this feminine energy will play a pivotal role in the Great Transition.

"So use your feminine qualities to navigate the waters ahead. Trust your intuition, be patient, gentle with yourselves and others, stay peaceful and strong.

Chapter 49

Leyla walked towards Li-ying, who was sitting in the lobby reading the paper. Her friend hadn't changed at all, she thought to herself. Still beautiful, her long black hair neatly tied back into a ponytail.

"Li-ying," she called out, and her friend jumped up to greet her. They hugged each other warmly for a few minutes, before sitting down. A waiter appeared as if from nowhere. They decided to order coffee before heading off to Hyde Park. Their walk in the park was a bit of a ritual for them; they did it every time they saw each other in London. As interns, it was a way for them to escape the stress and exhaustion of their daily routine.

"It has been too long," said Li-ying. The last few times Leyla had come to London Li-ying had been away at speaking engagements somewhere in the world. Her book, The Secret Power of Women, had been an instant best-seller and was now translated into 15 different languages.

"It has," replied Leyla. "I must tell you about this dream I had last night. Amazingly, some of it corresponds to what you wrote in your book, about women's power." Leyla also told her what the Elders at Chichen Itza had said, and about the messages that had been coming through in dreams to the people she had met there.

"In my dream, the Elder spoke about society's fear and distortion of women's innate creative and intuitive qualities, which has led to our repression and persecution through history."

Li-ying looked at her friend thoughtfully. "It's not just a fear of their inner creativity, it's a fear of the power of their sexuality," she said. "It's something that men can't control. The most extreme example can be seen in societies that practice circumcision as a way to repress and mutilate women."

"Why has this happened?" asked Leyla.

"My theory is that it is based on a primitive, possibly unacknowledged desire to maintain power within a patriarchal system," said Li-ying grimly. "This system exists in the majority of societies today. In the most primitive societies, women are severely oppressed and violently punished for 'disobedience'.

"You've seen cases where women who are raped through no fault of their own are then thrown into jail for their 'crime', which was inciting sexual desire. They are covered up to hide them from creating 'temptation'.

"During the barbaric European witch hunts of the Middle Ages," Li-ying continued, "thousands of women were tortured and murdered on ridiculous charges, which were largely the misogynistic sexual fantasies of the monks and priests who carried them out.

"In more 'civilized' society today, women are suppressed in more politically correct ways," she continued with a wry smile. "The objectifying of women in advertising as sex symbols is another way of degrading them and trivializing the true depth of their feminine power.

"Unfortunately, these perceptions have resulted in dysfunctional relationships between men and women. Instead of appreciating each other's strengths and weaknesses, many seem to either idealize or degrade each other.

"Some men in Western society have what they call a 'madonna–whore complex'," she added. "They feel that they can't be sexually fulfilled with the woman they love, the mother of their children. So they go to prostitutes, or get addicted to female porn on the Internet, to satisfy their so-called base desires."

"It is such a shame that this has happened," said Leyla, thinking of the wonderfully balanced relationship she shared with her husband Bahram. "Sex between two people on an equal yet complementary level, who love each other, can be the most wonderful experience in the world. It's almost spiritual. It's like a harmonious balance of male and female energies."

"They call that the balance of Yin and Yang," said Li-ying. In Chinese medicine, everyone has both Yin and Yang whether they are male or female. Yin is the feminine, quiet, and cool aspect of nature, linked with the Moon and Earth. Yang, linked with the Sun, is the masculine aspect of nature, active, bright, and expansive. The continued balance of Yin and Yang keeps the life energy, or 'Chi,' flowing through the body and life in general.

"I believe that that there is currently too much 'Yang' in the world," Li-ying said gravely. "This state of imbalance creates the delusion that we can live selfishly in constant conflict with others, and disregards our intrinsic connection with others and the Earth. Unfortunately, society tends to idealize people with too much Yang, such as the some of the aggressive movers and shakers.

"Distorted Yang is considered by Chinese medicine to be weak Yang, because it has little or no healthy Yin balance, especially because the Earth is Yin. It has been known to cause cancer and many other of the diseases we are experiencing today."

"How can this balance be redressed?" asked Leyla.

"According to Chinese medicine, the only way to correct this is to first strengthen the Yin," replied Li-ying. "Weak Yang, faced with a healthy, strong Yin, will also become healthy and strong. To strengthen our Yin, we need to turn within, and as the Sufi expression goes, 'polish the mirror of our Soul.'"

"Do you mean that society as a whole needs to focus on reconnecting with itself, and the Earth?" asked Leyla. "Adopt a 'female' attitude to business and politics?"

"Yes, but I doubt it would happen with the current people and systems in power," replied Li-ying. "Maybe women will take a temporary leadership role to redress the imbalance of male and female energy."

"Do you really see it happening anytime soon?" asked Leyla.

"I do think major shifts are happening already," replied Li-ying. "Although they are not affecting us directly just yet, they will start to very soon. We will know when these changes start to take place by the signs," she continued.

"Do you mean when the energy of power and control is withdrawn?" asked Leyla.

"Yes," replied Li-ying. "It is just a matter of time before the old system unravels, leaving space for a new and sounder base to build a new world. It will transform the world we live in, for the better."

Chapter 50

Leyla stretched out in the first-class bed on the aircraft and sighed contentedly. It had been a wonderful holiday, but it had gone too quickly. She grimaced in anticipation of returning to work. It wasn't that she didn't enjoy it. She just found it hard not to feel distressed by the misery and abject poverty of the peasant communities serviced by the hospital where they worked.

They had agreed to devote two years of their lives to underprivileged communities, before setting up private practice in Tehran. Their two years would be over in 6 months, and they would need to start planning their next steps.

Leyla started to think about what Li-ying had said about the plight of women. It was something she had never understood, as blind misogyny seemed irrational and completely unnecessary in her eyes. It was almost as if it were a hidden, subconscious fear that drove people to suppress and commit outrageous crimes against women.

She thought about the recent death of her colleague at the hands of the 'morals and virtues' police. What kind of society deemed it a crime to be in a public place with one's fiancée? It seemed more of an indication of a blind hatred of educated, powerful women, especially by the more primitive tribal communities steeped in local tradition.

I can't just sit back and watch this happen, Leyla thought to herself. She leaned over to Bahram, who was reading the paper.

"Bahram, I have had an idea about what we could do when we leave the hospital," she said. "I'd like to see what I can do to improve the status of women in our society."

Bahram frowned. "My dear, you are taking on a huge challenge, and you know it. The laws are changing, and the fundamentalists will not approve. But if it's really what you want to do, then of course I will support you."

Leyla smiled and took his hand. "Thank you, Bahram. It is something I really feel inspired to do. I am sure that with the right intention, I will succeed. The first thing I will do is get in touch with that top human rights lawyer, to see how I can start forming a network. I think that much of the problem lies with women themselves."

"What do you mean?" asked Bahram.

"We have been brainwashed for so long into thinking we are inferior that we actually believe it ourselves," replied Leyla. "If we don't empower ourselves, then nobody else can do it for us. We need to believe in ourselves."

Chapter 51

It was raining hard in London and Penny was tossing and turning, unable to get back to sleep. Finally, she drifted into a deep sleep and had a vivid dream.

"Here is the seventh and last message for your tribe.

"The world is about to undergo momentous change.

"Mother Earth is in the process of healing herself to bring Nature back into balance. The earthquakes, tsunamis, and hurricanes we are experiencing at an unprecedented level are designed to bring the planet back into harmony. The financial turmoil you are experiencing will only get worse.

"Prepare for this moment by living in the moment. Be mindful.

"Don't focus on the world of the past, which is polarizing towards selfishness and fear. Withdraw your attention and energy from the old media that keeps you conscious of global negativity and the crumbling society.

"A few fearful cities, where some of you are housed, may experience turmoil and distress. It may be the only way to stimulate the required change of heart, where love and education is not working.

"Some may die. Many will be disoriented. You will be needed to help guide people during this time, and help them recognize their true power to control and change the world around them.

"Any individuals or groups who continue to harbor selfish motives, or who work for organizations that exist solely to make personal profits, will find increasing tension, confusion, and conflict in their lives, becoming devitalized and debilitated.

"They may seek to tap your energy by using controlling methods of the past, trying to incite fear, anger, or anguish. This can come in unexpected ways. You will know when you keep focusing on a person or a problem you cannot seem to resolve. Remove your attention from them or you will be keeping them strong.

"Stay positive despite what happens around you, remembering it is all an illusion. Shift your attention to the world you want to live in, and away from the disasters around you. Live, feel breathe this new world and you will create it.

"It's up to you.

"You just need to focus your minds."

PART THREE

THE GREAT TRANSITION

'To obtain spirituality is to realize that the whole universe is one symphony. In this every individual is one note, and his happiness lies in becoming perfectly attuned to the harmony of the universe'

—Hazrat Inayat Khan, The Music of Life

Chapter 52

The sun had just started to rise in the morning sky, bathing the lush countryside in a soft yellow light. The tall sheaves of corn in the fields below seemed to be swaying, not to the wind, but to the exquisite tones of Mozart playing softly in the background.

It was the time of day that Aurelie loved the most.

A time when she could reflect in peace on the day ahead, and connect with herself. She was sitting outside on the terrace, contemplating the beauty around her, and sipping on a cup of freshly picked mint tea.

Sebastian appeared at the door, and walked over to give her a kiss. "The flight arrives at 9am," he said. "I'll pick the girls up and meet you back here at around 10.15."

Aurelie smiled contentedly. They were all coming to the Dordogne. It had been a year since they had met in Cancun, and much had been achieved since then.

Aurelie had moved into Sebastian's spacious farmhouse and had completed her first book, based on her experiences in Mexico. The book had made the best-seller lists in the US and UK and was now being translated into several foreign languages.

She had hardly told anyone where she was living, since discovering last year that her rented farmhouse had been fitted with surveillance equipment. Nobody knew that she had moved in with Sebastian except her inner circle. Even her parents thought she was back in Paris. The others had also moved house and continued their activities under assumed names, to avert suspicion.

Aurelie went back inside and ran up the stairs, only stopping to collect some sheets for the first bedroom.

Penny and Marianne were arriving first.

They had a lot to talk about. Marianne had been investigating the conflict of interest between the scientists advising WHO on the pandemic flu vaccine, and Penny had done some research into the electromagnetic fields surrounding all living beings, inspired by the work of several leading physicists such as David Bohm.

She had also set up an alternative network of scientists who refused to comply with the big business or pharmaceutical agenda, and helped source their funding from independent groups not as reliant on the selection process of 'peer review', which was more likely to be dominated by conservative viewpoints.

It's incredible how far we have come since we decided to question the status quo, thought Aurelie. *No wonder the 'unseen enemy' is worried about us. We are influencing more and more people to see the truth.*

Marianne had set up a UK-based team to monitor and raise consumer awareness of collusion between scientists and pharmaceutical companies following the H1N1 'swine flu' vaccination 'hysteria' in 2009.

She had widely promoted the fact that the Bureau of Investigative Journalism had found that three key scientists who advised the World Health Organization (WHO) about pandemic flu drugs had been paid by pharmaceutical companies Roche and Glaxo SmithKline for lectures, consulting work and research.

WHO had apparently been aware of this conflict of interest but did not disclose this information. What was worse was that the so-called 'pandemic' was never truly a pandemic, but only became one when WHO changed its definition in May 2009.

This made it no longer necessary for many people to get ill and die before a pandemic could be called. Now, the definition of a pandemic is a virus that spreads beyond borders and for which there is no immunity. As a result, countries were required to set up pandemic strategies and buy huge quantities of H1N1 vaccines and drugs that generated huge profits for the pharmaceutical companies involved.

Even the EU Health Committee had denounced WHO's actions, saying 'The definition of an alarming pandemic must not be under the influence of drug-sellers.'

Aurelie looked out of the window onto the undulating fields below. *Why were they so keen to vaccinate the human population?*

Chapter 53

The car pulled up outside the farmhouse and Aurelie ran out to greet it. Penny and Marianne jumped out and hugged Aurelie warmly, while Sebastian lifted the luggage out of the boot.

"It's so good to see you," said Penny. "What a lovely place," she continued, as her eyes looked around the surrounding fields of sunflowers and corn.

"We love it here," replied Aurelie. "As you know, I had to move very quickly from the place I was renting. I was being followed and monitored, as you were, and we needed to keep a low profile. According to everybody else I'm back in Paris living in my flat."

"Do you think they are still looking for you?" asked Marianne.

"Yes, and we have had a few near misses. Luckily Sebastian and I got together after I discovered the place was being bugged, so I don't think they know about our relationship. We keep out of the way here, most people don't think we know each other. "

The girls walked arm in arm into the large open plan sitting room.

"There is so much to talk about," said Penny.

Aurelie smiled. "I'll make you a cup of tea, then you can go and freshen up, because lunch will be ready soon." Aurelie had planned a small banquet for her friends, including locally produced pates, cheeses and terrines, accompanied by salad and crispy baguettes.

"When are the others arriving?" asked Marianne as she ran down the stairs. She eyed the food on the table and her mouth started watering. "This looks delicious – I can't wait!"

"Sit down," said Aurelie. "Everyone is arriving on a different day. Laurel, Jules, Campbell and Sam are arriving tonight. Trish, Yasmin, Guy and David arrive tomorrow. Leyla and Bahram arrive on Wednesday."

Penny walked down the stairs and gazed at the table appreciatively. "I'm starving," she said.

They all sat down and started lunch, delighted to be back together again.

"It's so nice to be here," said Penny. It's been a tough few months, but I'm glad to say we all seem to have made excellent progress."

"I agree," said Aurelie. "How is the project going?" she asked.

"Very well," replied Penny, serving herself a slice of terrine. "The most fascinating aspect of the work I'm researching is the concept of the universe as a huge energy exchange – a storage medium that the brain uses to retrieve information."

"I read the email you sent me about that book 'The Field' by Lynne McTaggart," said Aurelie. "After Guy mentioned it, I bought it and read it a few months ago. It is a fascinating proposition, I agree."

Sebastian nodded. "That book points to the huge body of evidence for the energy field. I'm just surprised that nobody seems to talk about it much on mainstream news. It is such an important concept, after all."

"I'm not surprised," said Marianne. "The media's main agenda is entertainment of the masses and they feed us what it suits them – and their masters – that we should know."

Penny looked around the table. "I'm feeding what I find through the alternative press, as well as through my own network. I am finding some skepticism but I keep going back to the facts. There simply isn't another theory that explains life as we know it."

"As Sebastian said, the implications are huge," said Aurelie. "If as these physicists suggest, we have the capability to change things by just focusing on them, then we could theoretically shift the world's primary driver from greed to good."

"Lynne McTaggart regularly conducts experiments based on changing situations through mind-power," said Penny. "She measures the results and there is always a connection. We most certainly have the ability to change our future outcomes. The most difficult thing is to actually believe it.

That afternoon, Marianne and Penny went for a walk while Aurelie and Sebastian prepared for the next wave of arrivals.

At around 5pm, a car pulled up in the drive. It was Laurel, Jules, Campbell and Sam. The three Australians had arrived in Paris from Sydney the day before and decided to overnight there, then met up with Jules before hiring a car and driving down to the Dordogne.

Sebastian heard the car and they all walked out to greet them. Campbell and Jules had been driving and looked tired, but Laurel and Sam looked surprisingly fresh considering their long journey.

"Welcome," said Aurelie warmly. "Come in, you must be exhausted!"

They showed them up to their bedrooms. Sam was sharing a twin room with Jules, and Campbell and Laurel had a lovely room with a four-poster overlooking the valley.

"Shall we meet on the terrace for aperitifs at around 6.30?" asked Aurelie. "Sounds great," they replied in unison.

A more relaxed trio emerged from their bedrooms at 6.30pm and went downstairs to the kitchen, where Aurelie was chatting to Penny and Marianne, who had returned from their afternoon walk. Penny's eyes lit up when she saw Sam, and they exchanged hugs all around.

Aurelie walked them out to the terrace, closely followed by Sebastian carrying a bottle of the local Pineau.

They sat down on the comfortable outdoor furniture and Sebastian started serving the aperitifs.

"How are your projects doing?" asked Marianne.

"Campbell and I have set up an organic farm in our community, using small scale, intensive and sustainable food production," replied Laurel. "The objective is to offer training in the setting up of local, community-based organic farms around the country, so that communities all over Australia can become sustainable."

"We finished the documentary on sustainable farming that will go to air in the next couple of weeks," added Sam.

"I have heard that there could be serious food shortages coming up, do you think there's any truth in that?" asked Penny.

"Freak weather, droughts and poor harvests are causing a global shortage in many basic foods, such as wheat, sugar, corn and even meat," replied Campbell. "This has also translated into unprecedented price rises," he continued.

Sebastian arched his eyebrows. "Has Australia been affected?" he asked.

"For the first time, Australia is importing more fruit and vegetables than it exports," Campbell continued. "Most of it comes from New Zealand, but recently a number of vegetables such as garlic, peas, cauliflower and beans are coming from China."

"The recent floods affecting most of Australia have also created a huge shortfall that will take some time to redress," he added.

Laurel got up and walked over to the edge of the terrace, and looked out at the undulating fields below.

"We need to find new approaches to deal with this resource scarcity and environmental change," she said. "I believe that in the future, people will source a much greater proportion of their essential needs from within their local communities. We need to break our reliance on multinationals, petrol and every aspect of the current society that is keeping us in 'chains'," she added.

"That's so true," said Aurelie. "Many of our local grocers and butchers have gone out of business, now that the supermarket chains have started to dominate the landscape. At least we still have our regular village markets, but fewer people are supporting them because the chains are so much cheaper."

Laurel nodded. "In the US, the government wants to introduce a bill to ban people from growing their own food."

"What?" said Penny.

"It's true," said Sam. "They are already trying to prevent small farms from growing organic foods, to protect the profits of large food producers who work on small margins. The bill Laurel's talking about is known as the S510, which will put all foods under the government of national security and defense."

Sebastian looked up. "Thank God that's not happening anywhere else, not yet anyway. We need more than anything now to start relying on our own resources, because the economic fabric of the world as we know it is on the brink of collapse."

Aurelie came out of the kitchen carrying a platter of hot chicken wings.

"Eat up guys," she said. "We don't know if we are going to have access to fresh foods for much longer," she added. "In any event, you are all welcome to come here, we have orchards full of fruit trees, as well as chickens, goats and cows."

They laughed.

"A reassuring prospect," said Sam. "Count me in."

Suddenly, Jules got up saying he had to go to the bathroom. He locked himself in and spoke quietly, making sure that nobody could hear the conversation.

"We are located in a farmhouse about 20 minutes from Brantôme, called La Reserve," he said. "No, they don't suspect. I'll keep you posted on our movements." He switched off his phone and went back out the back. Aurelie sensed there was something wrong, but put it down to resentment about Sebastian. Jules had never really got over the fact that they were now an item.

They ate dinner and continued to talk about the current state of world affairs, before retiring early in preparation for the next day.

Chapter 54

As Aurelie sat in the car on the way to the train station to pick up Guy and David, she thought about the implications of the seeming deterioration of the world financial system.

It had all started with the 'Credit Crunch' of 2008, followed by the collapse of equity markets in 2009, that had been propped up by the financial bailouts by countries around the world. The Middle East was experiencing constant rioting, and ongoing wars had generated further terrorist attacks around the world.

The mid-term elections in 2010 had increased the power of republicans in the senate, and the Fed injected a new amount of quantitative easing into the US economy, in face of world condemnation.

Maybe things are going to get better.

They arrived at the train station and Sebastian jumped out.

"Let's grab a cup of coffee before they arrive, we have time," he said. They walked into the small coffee shop near the station and ordered a coffee. As they walked in, Sebastian noticed a man sitting at a table by the door, who looked at them quickly before going back to his newspaper.

As they sat down, he whispered to Aurelie. "There's something odd about that guy, I can just feel it. We will have to take a detour home." They ordered coffees, drank them quickly then walked outside.

"You'd better go to the car and wait for me there," said Sebastian. "Don't go there directly, walk into the station with me, and get to the car park from the back entrance. Put a scarf on and drive the car up to that block of flats on the hill behind the coffee shop, I'll meet you with the guys up there in a few minutes."

Aurelie nodded and did what he asked. They had to be very careful, and even the slightest suspicion needed to be heeded.

About 10 minutes later, Sebastian appeared with Guy and David. They jumped quickly into the car and Sebastian drove off, keeping his eye on the rear mirror.

"It's great to see you both," said Aurelie. "Sorry about all the subterfuge. We have to be on alert, especially since we will all be together."

"We fully understand," replied Guy. "Ever since that trader from Golding Starks in London had a 'car accident' when he was going to spill the beans about what was really going on, we have been extremely careful as well."

"What do you mean?" asked Sebastian.

"He was going to reveal evidence that the big banks were manipulating the market, but was prevented from testifying in

Washington at the Commodities Futures Trading Commission. He did however send the information over to a Wall Street commodity broker who presented it on his behalf," replied Guy.

"The Commission pretty much cut him off, and the TV feed was censured so nobody really saw it. "He never lived to see the outcome," Guy continued. "The next day, he and his wife were hit by a car and both died instantly."

Aurelie shook her head in horror.

They arrived at the farmhouse using an alternative route, and Sebastian kept an eye on the rear view mirror just in case.

"Are we the first to arrive?" asked David.

"No," replied Aurelie as she took Guy and David up to their room. "Penny and Marianne arrived yesterday, Yasmin and Trish are driving down from Paris later today, and the others are arriving over the next few days. The girls are out canoeing this afternoon, so why don't you relax for a while then join us a bit later?"

"Sounds good," replied David as Guy nodded wearily.

Aurelie went down to prepare dinner for that evening. She decided to make a traditional 'cassoulet', a delicious combination of local sausage, chicken, vegetables and beans.

Sebastian came in and gave her a hug.

"Don't worry, we haven't done anything that would threaten them to that extent," he said reassuringly, knowing that she had been shocked by Guy's story in the car.

"Not yet," replied Aurelie with a frown.

At around 6pm, a car pulled up in the drive and Trish and Yasmin jumped out. Sebastian had given them strict instructions to take a different route if they thought they were being followed.

Aurelie and Sebastian walked out to greet them, and took them up to their room. "Where are the others?" asked Yasmin.

"Either asleep or canoeing," replied Aurelie. "We are meeting for drinks at 7pm downstairs, so take your time."

Sebastian and Aurelie went back downstairs, and Aurelie headed for the kitchen. "I'll put out the snacks if you get the aperitifs," she said.

A few minutes later, David and Guy came downstairs followed closely by Trish and Yasmin. Penny and Marianne came out to meet them from the kitchen. They greeted each other warmly, looking forward to spending a couple of weeks together to discuss their joint projects.

Sebastian took a bottle of champagne out to the seating area on the terrace, while Aurelie brought out a few snacks.

They sat down and gazed at the magnificent views. "What a lovely place," said Trish admiringly, as she stretched out on the couch. I thought South Africa had the most beautiful scenery in the world, but I'm starting to wonder," she continued.

"How have you been, Trish?" asked Aurelie. "I have been thinking about you a lot, especially since I have encountered a number of well-meaning, but in my opinion deluded people claiming to channel all sorts of information. Tell us about your project."

Trish smiled. "It has gained huge momentum," she replied. "I have set up global workshops linked around a website that discuss these issues openly. We are suggesting some critical techniques that people can use to be more discerning."

"Do you mean radars of a kind?" asked Penny.

"Yes, we are teaching people to use their intuition and start to build their own abilities, rather than looking up to others. It's a bit like religion, people have a tendency to believe and rely on others instead of relying on themselves," she added.

"That is so true," said Marianne.

"I am also working with children, the new Indigo and Crystal children who have a greater ability than most to cope with the changes at hand," said Trish.

"What kinds of abilities?" asked David.

"They are wired differently from us," replied Trish. "They can process over seven things at the same time, a generation of kids that can deal with a high rate of change and complexity to be able to deal with this new world. The current system is trying to medicate them, but they have a new set of skills that we should be working out how to use, because that's how we are going to survive in the future and shift from the old system to the new."

Guy looked pensive. "The old system is fighting hard to stay alive, but it's not succeeding. This latest round of Quantitative Easing, or the QE2 as they call it, may result in the collapse of the dollar, and will probably destabilize the world's financial system even further. It's just not sustainable, but it's the only thing they can do at this stage to buy time."

"Why won't it work?" asked Sebastian.

"Because it's just another bubble that will burst like the others did. It started with the dot.com bubble, then the real estate bubble, and now the 'bailout bubble' that is bigger than all of the bubbles combined! As the leading trends forecaster Gerard Celente says, they are 'dumping funny money into the system to keep it going'," said David.

"It will burst as well and the world economy will probably fail, it just can't be fixed," added Guy. "This is not about repairing an old and moribund system, it's about building something new and sustainable. It's now the time for people with the skills and intention to build a new world."

"What about the mid-term election change, will that make any difference?" asked Aurelie.

"Not really, because both the Republicans and Democrats obey the same master," replied Guy.

"Let me explain," said David. "In the past, Democrats were funded by the unions, while the Republicans represented business. Now that so many manufacturing and industrial jobs have been moved offshore, the unions don't have the finances any more, so the Democrats are dependent on the same source of financing as the Republicans. And as we all know, they do what their source of funding says."

"Is that why Obama hasn't stopped the war?" asked Yasmin.

"That's right. There's too much money and a hidden agenda there. They say that the continual aggression by US troops and mercenaries in the Middle East will lead to the next world war," said Guy.

"Some of the main supporters of US government election campaigns are investment banks, defense contractors and media agencies," added Guy. "How can they bite the hands that feed them?"

Aurelie and Sebastian went in to do the last minute preparations for dinner. They brought out dishes of honey chicken, roast potatoes and pan-fried courgettes, as well as a couple of fresh baguettes.

"Yasmin, how is your music program going?" asked Aurelie.

Yasmin smiled. "Very well," she replied. "Hundreds of musicians have signed up to the program, and we are being featured at the next Festival of Sacred Music. We have also set up a website with free downloads of inspirational music tracks, that are aimed at the young and not just the 'converted'."

"Congratulations," said Aurelie. "I can't wait for tomorrow to discuss the messages we have all been receiving," she added. "Music is definitely the theme that runs through everything we have learned. It is now gaining momentum as we draw closer to the Great Transition."

The midsummer sun set very late, and it stayed warm until almost 11pm. They ate dinner together out on the terrace, and watched the vivid sunset illuminate the horizon, before retiring to catch up on some well-needed sleep.

Chapter 55

The next morning Sebastian drove to the airport to collect Leyla and Bahram who were flying in from London. On the way back in the car, he asked her how her project to support Muslim women in the Middle East was progressing.

"It has been very challenging over the past few months," she replied with a frown. "We set up a blog to generate discussion of the key issues facing Muslim women and culture, approaching it in a peaceful, moderate way. We now have bloggers in several other countries who contribute information from their areas."

"Is it working?" asked Sebastian.

"From the point of view that it is less threatening than speaking out in public," replied Leyla. "But there is still a lot of fear. The government has arrested and jailed hundreds of women involved in peaceful civil rights protests over the past year. Many of them have been tortured and raped."

"The women of Iran have appalling human rights," added Bahram. "They don't have the right to choose their husbands, no right to education after marriage, no right to divorce, no right to child custody, no right to protection from ill-treatment in public places, and have restrictive quotas to universities. If they object to this, even peacefully, they are thrown into prison."

Leyla nodded her head silently. "One of our most prominent human rights lawyers is still on a hunger strike in prison and will probably die very soon," she said. "She was imprisoned for charges of 'acting against national security' when she has just been defending other human rights activists. She is one of many who have now been imprisoned on trumped up charges."

"That's terrible," said Sebastian. "But surely this will turn the corner with time?" he added.

"I would like to see a return to the freedoms that Islam brought women from the 7th to the 13th century, when so many women were scholars, poets and thinkers," she replied. "I am certain that we will get there eventually, even if things are not looking optimistic at the moment. This regime cannot continue to oppress us forever."

The car pulled up in the driveway, where Aurelie and the others were there to greet them.

At dinner that night, Guy brought up the issue of Iran's nuclear program. Bahram smiled ironically. "Iran belongs to the Nuclear Nonproliferation Treaty (NPT) and has not been granted Nuclear-Weapon State status under the NPT, exactly the same as

Brazil, Germany, Japan and the Netherlands," he said. "But I don't believe the government has any real interest in developing nuclear weapons," he added. "The likely reason why the US is threatening to bomb us is because they want to control the whole of the Middle East, and the Iranian government isn't playing ball."

"Because of the pipeline?" asked David.

"Amongst other things, yes. Look at what happened in Afghanistan," replied Bahram. "The US government had wanted a new government there since 1998, when plans for a natural gas pipeline were put in place. But they couldn't do it because it would have to run through Kandahar province, the heart of Taliban territory."

"Wasn't Dick Cheney a director of the US company involved?" asked Sam.

"Yes, and when the Bush-Cheney administration tried to negotiate with the Taliban in early 2001, they wanted more money than they were prepared to pay. So they threatened to bomb them instead," said Guy. "9/11 came at a convenient time."

"By claiming that Bin Laden was hiding out there in a cave, it enabled them to invade the country and get control that way," said Bahram. "It was also a way to flex muscle in the Middle East, under the pretext that it was controlling terrorism."

David laughed. "Hamid Karzai, the President of Afghanistan used to be a consultant for energy company Unocal, who were after the original pipeline contract. The irony is, the pipeline's nowhere near being completed, due to the problems with the Taliban, which seem to have gotten worse.

"So all that money, and all those lives, have so far been for nothing. Although nobody knows where the drug money from all the heroin the farmers are growing is going – although I have my suspicions," he added.

"Why are they threatening Iran?" asked Aurelie.

"Probably because Iran is not only OPEC's second largest oil producer, but has the world's second largest natural gas reserves," replied Bahram. "Pakistan signed an agreement with Iran for their pipeline, which will deliver natural gas from the Caspian Sea. Despite US concern, India is still thinking of joining."

"Is that because it would provide competition to their pipeline?" asked Aurelie.

"Absolutely," replied Bahram. "The US-backed pipeline would pipe natural gas from Turkmenistan and Uzbekistan into Pakistan and India. They would have major competition and from a 'non-friendly' country, and they'd rather have a monopoly to control prices."

Guy smiled. "So it's playing up the nuclear issue to try to delay negotiations. If they take over control of Iran by replacing the current government with one that serves US interests, then they can stop the pipeline from going ahead or take on the contract themselves. If they do go ahead and strike, they will use the nuclear issue as the reason to sell it to the public."

Chapter 56

The next day, the group gathered in the huge, tastefully-converted barn next to the house, where they planned to spend the day discussing and summarizing the insights they had gained over the past year.

They were also expecting Marie-Laure, a local musicologist and close friend of Aurelie and Sebastian.

They sat down around a large rectangular dining table that had originally belonged to the manor house nearby.

Aurelie stood up.

"Welcome everybody. I am delighted that you could all be here for this reunion," she said. "It has been a long and difficult journey, but we are now very close to the truth."

She walked over to the flip chart and picked up a crayon. "Why don't we start by summarizing the initial message from the Elders, and then the dreams?" she asked. The group nodded in agreement.

She started to write on the large sheet of white paper on the flip chart, as the group called out their suggestions.

A structure began to form and Aurelie summarized their conclusions on one sheet of paper, then sat down.

The group looked at the list. "It's hard to imagine how we could have compressed all that information onto one page," said Guy. "But we have."

MAJOR SHIFT IN 2012

a global transformation
end of 26,000 year cycle of evolutionary change
earth changes & turmoil signs of impending change

A VIBRATIONAL TRANSITION

world is created by collective human thought
ascension from 3rd to higher vibrational dimensions
through activation of dormant DNA

A BATTLE OF LIGHT AND DARK

beware "false prophets" ie some mediums etc
beware "dark side" who are trying to block ascension
use feminine qualities to win the fight ie love, intuition

SOUND IS THE KEY TO TRANSITION

strings of universal energy are raising their octaves
will resonate together to create a harmonious symphony
humanity must envision a positive future

"The sound issue is critical," said Yasmin. "The only thing I'm not sure of is if we need to be proactive in the process."

"I think it's going to be a combination of 'awareness' and proactivity," said Trish. "In other words, we need to spend time in nature, meditate, listen to our intuition – to be receptive to the transformational sounds. Eat healthy foods. And remain positively focused, in a state of gratitude for what we have, however small. If we don't, our vibrations may be too low to sense and absorb the changing octaves," she added.

"It's hard, though, given the complete mess the world is in at the moment," said David.

"That's the big challenge," said Marianne. "It's a question of choosing the world we want to live in."

"But so many people are living in fear," said Penny. "It's all very well for us, sitting in beautiful surroundings in the middle of the countryside. It's easy for us to meditate and feel calm about it all, we aren't homeless or in distress."

"That's why we need to keep the vibrations high for everybody else," said Aurelie. "If just 10% of the population keeps them high then we can pull the rest of the world with us."

"It could get harder for us too," said Sebastian. "We need to be particularly vigilant, but we are now aware, and are spreading the message. It will be a question of focusing on a positive outcome despite what is going on around us. That way, we can jump into another timeline, another dimension."

"Believing it is the hardest," said Jules. "It's such a radical change from anything we have been taught."

"True," replied Aurelie. "But we have heard this from so many sources now, and theoretical physicists believe that it is the most likely explanation for the world we live in. So it is no longer the realm of fantasy. It has become fact."

They broke for lunch. Aurelie and Penny had cooked up a delicious feast of creamy chicken and mushroom pasta, quiche, salads and Moroccan lemon cake for dessert.

That afternoon, Marie-Laure was planning a session on sound. She walked over to the flip chart and wrote out a quote from Rudolph Steiner:

'There will come a time when a diseased condition will not be described as it is today by physicians and psychologists, but it will be spoken of in musical terms, as one would speak of a piano that was out of tune.'

She turned back to the group. "Now that we know that the human body is made up of vibrating molecules, we understand how sound healing works," she said.

"I have used it in my practice for many years as the ancients did in the past" she said. "I use crystal bowls, an Australian didgeridoo, bells and drums, all these instruments work together to recalibrate the vibrations in the human body, and restore them to an optimum vibrational level."

"The messages we have been receiving keep leading back to sound being the key to humanity's ascension," said Aurelie.

"That's right," replied Marie-Laure. "I think that we are on the verge of finding the key that will heal humanity and move it out of its vibrational prison. Our world has become discordant, and so have we. We need to recalibrate our vibrational structure and restore it to its original blueprint."

"How will we do that?" asked Penny.

"Tomorrow we will go to the sacred cave and meditate," she replied. "It was specially revered by the Druids, because it houses a natural spring and is on the bank of a fast-moving river."

Aurelie looked up. "I had a message about it in a meditation. I saw a huge diamond crystal embedded in the ground below it," she said. "It had been anchored there eons ago by the ancients, who also charged it with pure white energy that emanates through the ley lines that cross it."

"Is it a portal?" asked Trish.

"Most definitely so," replied Marie-Laure. "By meditating there, we will be able to amplify any energy that we draw through the portal into the earth below. We can also channel it through the energy grid by harnessing the power of the crystal."

Aurelie added. "I am sure that our answer lies there."

Chapter 57

The next morning, they set off for the cave, driving past several magnificent fields of sunflowers. After parking the cars, they walked through a small forest before arriving at the cave, which was right next to the river.

Marie-Laure stood outside the cave. "Before we go in, I'd like to tell you the story of this cave and of the Druids that revered it," she said. "The Druids were at one with nature and the seasons. Like many 'primitive' people, they saw spirituality in the simple things, like the sunrise, natural springs, the music of the earth.

"We need to return to that time, and reconnect with each other and the earth," she said. "Stretch out and greet the morning sun, run through the fields, swim in the rivers, and meditate to hear the voice within."

She beckoned the group to follow her into the cave. They looked around in awe at the magnificent stalagtites and stalagmites, and the pool of crystal clear water. They put several blankets and cushions over a huge tarpaulin and lit a few candles.

Marie-Laure had brought her 'OHM' tuning fork with her and explained how she would use it. "The OHM is considered to be the original, primordial sound from which all other sound emanates," she said. "It was known by the ancients to be the most powerful vibration. Aurelie will activate it during the meditation.

"I will now close my eyes and await a channeled message[10]," she continued. "Sit with crossed legs and with your backs straight. Close your eyes, breathe deeply several times, then slow your breath down," she said.

"Call a column of white light to you now from the heart of the galaxy. Tune into your aura and open your 12th chakra above your head, and your 1st chakra below you, and feel this beautiful white light flowing through you, and raising your vibrations. Send a grounding cord down into the heart of the core crystal of the Earth, and experience a feeling of connection with her.

"Now ask for any energy you have ever given away, or left behind, be returned to you. When it has returned, ask the angels to send a cascade of golden energy down through your aura, and call unconditional love to yourselves. Spin this golden light around you and seal yourselves in it, and ask for your 12 chakras and 12 DNA strands to be reconnected.

"See your DNA spinning like healthy spirals of light in each cell of your body, and your 12 chakras spinning together. See every molecule in your bodies vibrate at a higher level, as you resonate with the sounds of the universe. Hear the individual notes that you play as part of your role in the universal symphony, and

---

10 Inspired by **www.solara.org.uk**

recalibrate your beings to this primordial sound. You are now part of the Great Universal Symphony."

Marie-Laure opened her eyes and looked around at the group. There was an incredible energy in the space.

"We have the answer we were looking for. We need to "retune" ourselves and find our unique primordial sound, so that we can join in the harmony of universal creation," she said. "We need to meditate as groups in powerful energy centres, and send our positive thoughts out to the universe. This was what the Elders were trying to tell us."

She looked around the cave. "Now that we are fully energized, and harnessing the power of the diamond crystal beneath us, let us visualize the world we want to see in the future, and send this vision through the 'ley lines'," she said.

They group closed their eyes and imagined their perfect world.

Society was based on ethical principles, fairness, and abundance for all. There was no need for war, because everybody had what they wanted. There was no longer any poverty. Alternative, natural energy sources provided all the power they needed.

People were able to pursue their dreams without any constraints, because the universe materialized what they wanted. They were reunited with their soul mates. Communities lived in sustainable harmony with the earth and her resources. The world was at peace.

Chapter 58

Before getting back into their cars, Aurelie suggested that they take a walk along the river, to enjoy some of the spectacular scenery in the area. Sebastian went back to pick up his camera from the car.

They heard him running back, and Aurelie stiffened. "Quickly, we need to get out of here," he said. "I checked the underside of the cars and someone has wired them with explosives. They have caught up with us."

Aurelie had an immediate intuition. She looked at Jules. "Have you betrayed us?" she asked. He hung his head.

Sebastian went up to him and grabbed his arms, pinning them behind him and taking his mobile phone. He was in control, but his fury could be seen behind his calm demeanour.

"Sam, get some rope from the car. Get some of the biscuits out of the boot too. Aurelie, contact "our friend" on your pay as you go mobile and ask him to come and collect us. Leave all the other mobiles behind or they'll be able to track us. I will take Jules to a safe place and secure him, giving us enough time to get away. He'll survive for a few days."

Sebastian dragged Jules off and tied him up securely in a nearby cave. "I'll let someone know where you are in a few days," he said. "Although after what you did, you don't deserve to live."

He went back to the group and they set off for their rendezvous, covering their tracks along the way. Jean, a farmer they knew in the area, met them further up the river and piled them all into the back of his truck, covering them with a tarpaulin. Sebastian had told him months ago about the danger they may be in, and they had planned this escape route just in case.

Jean drove them to his farmhouse, and took them straight into his large barn, which he had partially converted to house seasonal labourers. There were several beds scattered around, and a shower room. "Make yourselves comfortable," he said. "Marie will bring you some supper shortly. Nobody will suspect you are here."

They all sat down and looked at each other. "I can't believe he did this," said Aurelie.

Sebastian put his arm around her. "I know. Don't worry, we will get through this. In a couple of days we will move to Francois' house. He is living in New York now and only comes over occasionally. It is stocked with food and provisions. We will stay under the radar until we can get everybody home."

Chapter 59

The rain lashed relentlessly at the window as thunder and lightning filled the night sky. Aurelie looked out the window, wishing Sebastian would get home.

It's cold, she thought as she put a couple of extra logs on the fire. She poured herself a glass of wine and sat in the huge armchair next to the fireplace, looking at the dancing flames.

The changes are starting.

The turmoil and unrest in the Middle East had increased the price of oil, causing huge increases in the price of food and other necessities. After the collapse of the monetary system in the autumn of that year, the government had started to impose some restrictive new systems, including a cashless society.

They had decided that the best way to avoid a future financial crisis was to introduce a single global currency and a single electronic card that served not only as an ID card, but could access all financial holdings.

It was compulsory. Aurelie hated the idea that she had no choice, but unfortunately there was now a monopoly in the banking system, so she would not be able to buy anything without the card. Initially, she had not minded the idea of it, reasoning that the government knew everything they wanted to know about her anyway.

But there seemed to be a sinister new agenda. Using the excuse of identity fraud, which had seen a dramatic rise recently, the card was now being replaced by an electronic chip. Penny had warned her about the effect of microchip implants.

It was bad enough that they could tag your movements, but it also meant that you were electronically connected to a computer. Penny had explained that as the body is an electromagnetic entity, the chip would allow manipulation through centralized computer control.

Luckily, the process was taking some time as city dwellers were being tagged first. Aurelie and Sebastian were going to try to avoid being tagged altogether. Their friends in the local community felt much the same, so they were working out a local barter system that would avoid the necessity of joining the scheme.

After all, they could live quite adequately without money, as long as they could get what they needed locally.

The rest of them were doing the same thing.

After the incident at the cave, they had moved to Sebastian's friends' farmhouse and the visitors had all managed to get home. To maintain a low profile for the time being, they had "dropped out" of society.

Penny and Sam, along with Marianne, had moved to Cornwall and created a sustainable, barter-based community. Laurel and Campbell had done the same in Wollombi, their country town near Sydney.

Leyla and Bahram were living in a community outside Tehran. Yasmin, Carlo, and Manuela were still in Buzios, but developing a barter-based community there.

Trish had set up a community just inland from Cape Town, and Guy and David had done the same in Cape Cod.

They were determined not to be reliant on the system, because they were not at all sure of the implications. They all knew at this stage, however, that it did not have their welfare, or the welfare of humanity, at heart.

Chapter 60

That night, Aurelie had an extraordinary dream. She dreamed that she had met a version of herself who lived in the future, who came back to tell her what was yet to happen and give her the inspiration and clarity to finish her second book.

In her dream, she was sitting by the grotto near the farmhouse and looking into its deep green waters. Suddenly, a being who looked a little like her, but wasn't her, came up through the water and sat next to her on the rock.

She began to speak to her telepathically.

"Aurelie, my name is Aura, and I am a part of you from the future. I have come back in time to help you understand the major shift you are about to experience.

"I am a time traveller, able to move forwards and backwards at will.

How can you travel through time? thought Aurelie.

"Time is related to frequency," Aura replied. "In the same way that a musical chord is composed of several tones, the universe is composed of several dimensions, each vibrating at a particular frequency. You are currently in the third dimension, a frequency where time is linear, with a distinct past and future that overlap the present. In higher dimensions, the present is greatly expanded, as the partitions between past and future are easily collapsed. As a result, I am able to travel through time, as you will as well, in the future.

Aurelie wondered how she had got there.

"The Earth's shifts and changes have opened up a number of dimensional portals, of which this is one," she replied. "This has resulted in a thinning of the veil that divides you from the 4th and higher dimensions.

Why are you here? asked Aurelie.

"You are poised at the threshold of a whole new cycle of evolution," replied Aura. "What is happening here on Earth is creating a ripple effect throughout all creation. You are nearing the end of a 25,920 year cycle to begin an entirely new one, marked by the Precession of the Equinoxes. You are in the process of being exposed to a high-vibrational stream of light emanating from the centre of the galaxy, which will synchronize the entire galaxy with the eternal Spirit of the Creator.

"Hindu scriptures describe this new cycle as the "Inbreath of God," which follows the "Outbreath of God" that we have experienced for almost 26,000 years. In that moment of time between the In- and Outbreaths, the veils of the dimensions will disappear, allowing the loving consciousness of Spirit to infuse the entire universe.

What will happen then? asked Aurelie.

"At that moment of infusion, the frequency of the entire planet will be raised in a sudden awakening, moving you collectively into the fourth dimension and beyond.

Do we all make the transition? asked Aurelie.

"Some of humanity does, and some does not," replied Aura. "What keeps changing is the actual proportion. In an optimum scenario, all beings on the planet will move up to the 5th dimension. In a second scenario, there will be a split between the worlds, and those who are not willing to move up will remain to play out their karma on a parallel Earth.

How can we make sure that we make the transition? asked Aurelie.

"You must unify both shadow and light and experience Oneness," she replied. "Recognize that the darkness is as part of you as the light, and neither can exist alone. Accept yourselves. Extend forgiveness and love to all, not just to your loved ones, but also those you despise and fear. Be grateful for everything you have. Doing this will bring to an end the polarized conflict and lead to a complete planetary awakening.

"Importantly, recognize the creative power of your thoughts, as it is a power far beyond what you realize. Understand that you and your external existence are just an interpretation of your thoughts. If your attention is fragmented, you are fragmented.

When your attention is in the past, you are in the past. When your attention is in the present, you are in the presence of God.

"Release identification with the past and future, and live in the present. See guilt and fear for what they really are. Imagine that you are a huge inflatable membrane, designed to be filled to the full with the energy and power of life. Like two enormous rips in each side, guilt and fear allow the precious energy of life to disappear, leaving you withered while you use your life substance to energize everything that you fear. Wake up, and stop handing over your power. This is all an illusion.

"Trust in what happens, and don't get caught up in the drama. If things don't go as you expect, wait with trust and don't get upset or anxious. The design will be revealed in every situation, and specific information will be supplied to you constantly.

"Be attentive.

"Remember," continued Aura, "you are not alone. Call on your angels, guides, the ascended masters, your higher selves, Christ, and all manifestations of the great Spirit to help you. We will join with you to achieve this wonderful task, and be with you when the Golden Age begins."

Aura kissed Aurelie on the cheek then disappeared back into the green waters of the lagoon.

Chapter 61

Newsflash....November 2nd, 2012: A series of gamma ray bursts, emanating from the centre of our galaxy, has caused an overload of many global power lines and satellites, causing electricity blackouts all over the world. As most of Western technology is dependent on computer chips, it has brought civilization as we know it to a standstill.

A horrifying side effect is the apparent short-circuiting of people and animals that have been inserted with electronic microchips. Fortunately, only a small percentage of the world's population has been fitted with the devices to date. Scientists have been warning of the possibility of gamma ray blackouts for some time, ever since they discovered that the 2004 tsunami was followed by the brightest gamma ray burst recorded in recent history.

It was noted that the rays had disturbed some of the global satellites. The tsunami itself would have been caused by a gravity wave that normally precedes the gamma ray. Gravity waves have the potential to induce significant tidal forces that can cause earthquakes and shifts in the polar axis.

While gamma ray bursts have always occurred, they have been increasing in frequency and intensity for the past 10 years.

The last time a major gamma ray superwave hit the Earth was approximately 13,000 years ago, at the end of the last ice age.

It caused dark clouds of cosmic dust to engulf our solar system and dramatically altered the Earth's climate, causing the polar ice caps to melt suddenly, resulting in cataclysmic flooding. It also disrupted the Earth's magnetic balance, causing a reversal of the magnetic poles. Scientists have shown that what they call "galactic core explosions" actually occur about every 13,000–26,000 years.

Aurelie read the newsflash with a sense of dread. *It's all happening*, she thought. She quickly typed out an email and sent it to the group to see whether they were OK, and if they still had electricity and communications.

After about half an hour, she received replies from Laurel, Trish, and Penny. They said that they were still receiving power in parts of the country, but that they were using generators for electricity to power their fridges and lights. Laurel and Penny's broadband was no longer working, so they were using dial-up instead.

A few minutes later, an email appeared from Guy:

Hi Aurelie, thanks for your email. We've just had news that a huge hurricane has struck the Texas oil refineries, crippling oil production from the region. Storms have also dumped more than 20 cm of rain over the Midwest, causing even more flooding in our grain-growing region. U.S. crop damage has already hit $8 billion this year, and they are saying it is causing the worst flooding in 15 years. It's going to affect supplies of basic foodstuffs quite severely. We are OK, our community is holding together. Thank God we avoided being chipped.

Aurelie returned to her computer to read more on the latest news.

In addition to the global electronic blackouts, a sudden spate of seismic activity has caused tsunamis in various parts of the world. Although communications are down in these areas, information is emerging that parts of Eastern Australia, Indonesia, and Thailand have been hit by massive tidal waves that have devastated much of the coastline.

New reports are emerging that the gamma ray activity had caused an acceleration in the melting of the polar ice caps, which had already started deteriorating because of global warming. Scientists estimate that within as little as 2 weeks, coastal areas that are less than ten meters above sea level will be covered with water. As almost 40% of the world's population lives in coastal areas, the ramifications could be severe. Apart from losing their homes, coastal communities could lose up to 50% of their fresh water supplies due to the intrusion of salt water into groundwater channels.

Countries at particular risk are China, India, Bangladesh, Vietnam, Indonesia, Japan, Egypt, the United States, Thailand, and the Philippines. However, the countries with the largest share of their population living within 10 meters of the average sea level are the Bahamas, Suriname, Netherlands, Vietnam, Guyana, Bangladesh, Djibouti, Belize, Egypt, and Gambia. Major financial hubs like New York and London are also at risk, because parts of the cities are located below sea level.

Aurelie heard Sebastian's car pull up in the drive. She rushed outside and he took her into his arms. "Did you hear the news?" she asked him.

Sebastian nodded gravely. "We thought this might happen," he said. "But, then, change tends to happen only when things go terribly wrong.

"Now is the time to put into practice what we have been telling the others," he continued. "We have to keep a vision of a positive outcome and trust that everything is as it should be.

"We need to keep fear at bay, because as co-creators we have the opportunity to change the future, and create a brighter one for us all."

He stroked Aurelie's hair. "Don't worry, this will pass. We will get through it more easily if we just surrender to the flow, and keep meditating on our vision of the new world, so that we can shift dimensions and leave the old world behind.

"These are the signposts for the Great Transition."

PART FOUR

THE NEW WORLD

We are what we think.

All that we are arises with our thoughts.

With our thoughts, we make the world.

—Buddha

Chapter 62

2015: 3rd-Dimensional Earth

Jonathan hopped onto the shuttle that would take him back to his house in Washington County, New York. He was hungry and tired after a long day of meetings with representatives from the New World Government, who had come to the Unites States to meet with local government representatives.

There was still a lot to be done.

The 2011–2012 disasters had claimed the lives of almost three quarters of the world's population. Rising sea levels had enveloped large parts of the world's surface, so survivors were living at least 30 m above sea level.

Much of New York City was now under water, so survivors had moved to the lower slopes of the Adirondack Mountains. Africa had survived the events far better than other continents, given its geographical location near the equator and areas of low seismic activity. Johannesburg was the capital of the New World Government.

To control the large groups of homeless who were running amok all over the habitated world, military patrols were now monitoring the streets within the gated security areas. *It's like living in a police state*, Jon thought grimly.

Jon finally arrived at his house, waved at the security guard, and unlocked the gate by waving his arm over the built-in scanner. The chip in his right arm served a multi-functional purpose, from holding credits, to controlling security access programmed for his approved level.

Once inside the house, he switched on the light. The photo of his wife and children greeted him as he walked in. They had been killed during the hurricane, and the sadness he still felt was indescribable.

Jon went to the fridge and took out a beer. He was glad that that he had stocked up on provisions—you never knew when things were going to run low. Beers were a luxury to be drunk on a special occasion. He felt that he deserved a treat after such a hard day.

He sat down on his lounge chair and switched on the TV. The news was showing footage of the military police rounding up homeless and carting them away in large trucks. Jon was never sure where they were being taken, but on one level, he didn't really care as long as it was away from him.

As he sipped his beer, he wondered what had happened to his friends Guy and David. They must have gone during the hurricane. *I should have taken more notice of what they were saying*, Jon thought.

He stood up and walked over to the window, looking out at the barbed wire on his fence and the desolate landscape beyond. The Earth finally got her own back. And boy, Big Brother really is alive and kicking. He sighed wearily.

What a life.

Chapter 63

2015: 5th-Dimensional Earth

Elan, Joyelle, à table!

The two children stopped playing and ran through the French doors into the farmhouse kitchen where Aurelie was placing a steaming dish of baked aubergines onto the table. She had also prepared a fresh salad using tomatoes and lettuce freshly picked from the garden.

Sebastian walked in from the sitting room with a bottle of St. Emilion in his hands. He pulled the corkscrew out of the drawer and opened it with a pop, before pouring two full glasses, and two half glasses for the children.

Aurelie kissed him on the cheek and sat down at the table. Conversation was so much easier these days, she thought, as she told him how good the wine was. He smiled and replied that it was one of the best vintages of the decade. He said he had picked it up in town on his way home.

They ate their dinner while music played in the background; it was one of the tunes that Yasmin's School of Sacred Music had composed. It was a wonderful album, because it had a contemporary sound with the uplifting "phi" element of the genre. The sun set slowly behind the trees, and Aurelie felt completely and utterly happy.

Life was so much better. The world they had envisioned had materialized. Society was no longer based on greed, but rather on ethical principles, and sustainability. The negativity had disappeared.

She thought back to her time in Mexico, before the amazing adventure had begun. She wished that she could reunite with her old friends. It would be wonderful to stay in that beautiful villa that Trish had rented, all together, for an evening.

Suddenly, she found herself on the Riviera Maya, at the same villa she had remembered.

They were all there.

Trish was glowing and had brought her new partner William, a handsome, rugged man in his late fifties who obviously doted on her. Joshua and Indigo had met up with Elan and Joyelle, and were playing with them on the beach.

Penny and Sam were holding hands by the pool, smiling broadly. Penny looked a good eight months pregnant, and incredibly happy. Marianne was there as well, with her new partner John.

Guy and David walked over and gave her a hug, and shook hands with Sebastian. "I'm so glad to see you," she said.

Aurelie took Sebastian's hand and walked over to Yasmin, who looked beautiful in a white, off the shoulder dress. She had married Marco just a few weeks before, and they had dropped in from their honeymoon. She hugged them, then walked up to Laurel and her partner Campbell with Sebastian.

Leyla and Bahram walked over and hugged her warmly.

She felt wonderful. Life was so good, so joyful, so fulfilled.

Nothing could spoil it. All the negativity, fear, control, guilt, unhappiness, jealousy, and anxiety had gone with the shift into the 5th dimension. There simply wasn't any room for it any more. It didn't belong in this new world.

It was as it was always meant to be. A glorious symphony of life, in all its beauty.

ANGELA CLARKE

Angela Clarke has written several technical and historical non-fiction books, but 2012 The Symphony is her first novel. The 1st edition was published in 2008, and she has added new material and an additional 90 pages to the 2nd edition.

Before becoming a writer, Angela worked as a business consultant, after graduating with a Masters degree in business and marketing. She enjoys a varied lifestyle and travels regularly, drawing inspiration from the places she visits. She currently lives in London and spends part of the year in France.

CPSIA information can be obtained at www.ICGtesting.com
Printed in the USA
LVOW061707200512

282488LV00008B/16/P